Deadly Care
A Claire Burke Mystery
(Book 6)

by
Emma Pivato

This book is fiction. All characters, events, and organizations portrayed in this novel are the product of the author's imagination or are used fictitiously. Any resemblance to actual persons—living or dead—is entirely coincidental.

Copyright 2016 © by Emma Pivato

All rights reserved. No parts of this book may be reproduced or transmitted in any form or by any means, electronic or mechanical, including photocopying, recording or by any information storage and retrieval system, without written permission from the author, except for the inclusion of brief quotations in a review.

For information, email **Cozy Cat Press**, cozycatpress@gmail.com or visit our website at: www.cozycatpress.com

COZY CAT PRESS

ISBN: 978-1-946063-09-0
Printed in the United States of America

10 9 8 7 6 5 4 3 2 1

This book is dedicated to my dear friend,

Elena Roncucci

Elena is everything I ever wanted to be. She is smart and talented and kind and patient – an accounting whiz, a brilliant housekeeper and a skilled and gracious hostess. Elena listens without judging and guides without pushing. She is a true and faithful friend.

I wish to once again acknowledge the ongoing support of my husband, Joe Pivato, who carefully read through the manuscript and made many helpful suggestions.

I would also like to thank my long time friend, Kathy Talwar, for her very thorough proofreading and discovery of numerous typos.

Prologue

Was it a dream? At first it seemed like something soft and warm was snuggling against her. Her baby? But against her nose—why her nose? It was getting hard to breathe. And there was no baby smell...and no baby sounds. No sounds at all. Oh! She couldn't breathe! And then someone was speaking in a loud voice and there was no more pressure. She opened her eyes a tiny crack and saw a dark shadow moving away.

Chapter 1: Claire Comes to a Turn in the Road

Claire was depressed. Actually, she was depressed, annoyed and angry. Most of all she was angry—and demoralized. It had been three months since their last murder case. But that was a good thing, surely? One should not regret a lack of murders because one was bored. And Claire realized that she needed to add 'bored' to her list of angsts.

I'll clean out the kitchen cupboards, she thought. Today was Claire's day off from working with Roscoe at the home she had brought into being. Well, more aptly, she had *bulldozed* it into being with the help of friends, family and anyone else she could rope into the project. Now it served three adults. There was Roscoe, a kind and gentle young man with Down syndrome and a penchant for coconut cream pie. And there was Bill, who coped with autism and a significant cognitive disability. He was alternately fascinated with the knife tossing showmanship of his chef friend, Satou Botan, and the non-verbal messages of his elusive girlfriend, Mae-Mae, known to the rest of her world as Mavis. Mavis was the third roommate in their shared home and, while she could not talk, what she *did* have was a mysterious Mona Lisa-like smile that kept Bill guessing and continually entranced.

Claire had been running the new home since it had started almost two years ago and for a long time, the little community that had built up around it had been struggling with what to call it. 'Group home' seemed too impersonal, but referring to it as 'Roscoe's, Bill's and Mavis's home' was very awkward. Finally, their neighbor, Amanda, had suggested 'Co-op,' because it certainly had been a cooperative effort.

"Too common!" Claire's Aunt Gus had objected.

But Claire had not agreed. "Common is good," she'd argued. "Common, ordinary, everyday—normal. It's just another house in the neighborhood that happens to be set up a little bit differently. That's what we're aiming for!"

Claire opened her cell phone and pulled up a definition of 'co-operative' from the Internet and read it out for the others to hear.

"Based on the principles of empowerment, education, and community, co-ops operate laterally, promoting participation both within their own organization, and through a focus on community interaction, and support."

After Claire said this, the rest of the group agreed and soon it became quite easy and comfortable to simply refer to the home as 'the Co-op'.

Claire thought back to all that their little group had been through together. First, there had been the challenge of getting Bill acquitted of a murder charge only to find there was no place for him to go once he'd left the locked hospital ward where he was being held. That had been the reason for developing the Co-op in the first place.

Then, just when things were falling into place, Roscoe had witnessed the murder of a friend and had been seen by the murderer who later targeted him. Keeping Roscoe safe and finding the killer had absorbed the energies of the entire group, and placed Tia in serious danger.

Other adventures had followed, most recently tracking down the murderer of Bill's Aunt Marion. That had been a real nightmare and everyone—including Claire—had been very relieved to return to a quiet regular life once it was over. But now? Now there were only the endless hours of training and drilling Roscoe's math calculation skills, Bill's social skills and Mavis's physical skills. And Claire realized that she was becoming bored.

She thought about the restaurant. That was still a source of satisfaction. Roscoe had been deeded it as compensation for the trauma he had experienced. Claire smiled when she thought of the incredible process the friends and family of Roscoe, Bill and Mavis had gone through to turn the rather seedy fish and chips cafe into an elegant Japanese-Canadian fusion restaurant where both Bill and Roscoe had been able to find meaningful work.

Remembering their struggles to get the restaurant refurbished and up and running brought to mind Marisa, the mother of her close friend, Tia. Marisa had contributed so much with her sewing skills and Italian culinary expertise. She and her Italian-Canadian friends had worked side by side with Roscoe's Japanese family and had learned to appreciate each other's tastes and talents in the process. *What a wonderful experience that was!* Claire thought to herself wistfully. But then her happy memories curdled.

Marisa—vibrant, lively, gifted Marisa—had recently suffered a stroke, and after spending two weeks in the University Hospital was now in an extended care placement. Paralyzed, confined to a wheelchair and no longer able to attend to her most basic functions independently, she was living a terrible life. And so was her husband, Alberto, left on his own and not knowing how to help her or how to cope. And Tia, poor Tia! She was suffering agonies of guilt, but helpless to do much for her mother as she had her five-week-old baby girl to care for, who might be having some problems of her own.

But it didn't have to be this way, Claire thought angrily. Marisa did not need to be in the rehab hospital—all dignity stripped away, nothing to look forward to, no reason even to go on living. It could be so different. She thought then of her pet project and of the cold reception it had received from government officials, wheelchair companies and public health professionals. *Their answer was better, was it?* Claire asked herself through gritted teeth. But just then the ringing phone interrupted her angry thoughts.

"Claire, its Tia. I know it's your day off but would you have time to visit my mother? I just can't risk taking Marion there and Jimmy is working late today." After a pause, Tia added, "I'm worried about la mamma." And Claire could hear the slight sob in her voice.

Claire looked around her kitchen, which was in total disarray. And as she spoke, she thought quickly. "Uh, I was in the middle of cleaning the kitchen cupboards, but you know how much I like cleaning! I'll just finish the top cupboards so I can put everything away and leave the bottom ones for another day. It'll take me about an hour and I'll leave then. Will that be okay?"

"Thank you, Claire. That will be great! Oh, and I have a new picture of Marion for my mother. Could you pick it up on your way?"

"No problem. But Jessie will be home at four so I can't stay too long. Mia told me she has a dental appointment at two and might arrive a little late." Jessie was Claire's 14-year-old daughter. Although she had a severe disability, Jessie travelled back and forth from school on a special bus, and her assistant, Mia, arrived at four each school day to care for her until eight.

"Thanks! But I hope you'll be able to come over for a short while after your visit to tell me how my mother is. I have your favorite apple cake."

"I'll try. If not, I'll phone you later with an update."

Chapter 2: Hospital Life

When Claire entered St. Jerome Extended Care Hospital, the first thing she noticed was the smell. It was the sad human smell of old people caged together with diminishing control of their bodily functions and limited bathroom access. It made her angry and depressed at the same time—angry about the rigid and unimaginative hospital structure and protocol, and depressed about poor Marisa being reduced to this situation.

Claire struggled to regain control of her emotions and that process was made somewhat easier by the smiling face of the receptionist. She greeted Claire warmly and asked who she was there to see.

Claire was never one to hide her feelings and she blurted out her disgust and sadness about the smell. The woman, whose name was Alma according to her nametag, nodded her head sympathetically, and the woman's kind response helped Claire to put on a happy face before entering Marisa's room and greeting her.

Claire had not seen Marisa for a while because before her stroke Marisa had lived with her husband, Alberto, in Wetaskiwin, a small town 70 kilometers south of Edmonton. *I wonder if she will recognize me,* Claire worried to herself. Marisa was lying flat on her back in her bed, her wispy hair fanned out across the pillow. With a shock, Claire observed that the roots were growing out in a patchwork of dark and white. All her previous memories of Marisa involved a lady who was immaculately groomed.

"Hello, Marisa. Do you remember me...Claire?" There was no response. "Tia asked me to give you this," Claire added, holding out an enlarged photograph. "This is a new picture of your granddaughter, Marion Marisa. She's five weeks old now!"

Marisa continued to look straight ahead and the expression on her face did not change. Claire was beginning to wonder if she was more damaged than the doctors had thought, but then she saw a silent tear slipping out of Marisa's eye.

"Tia really wants to bring the baby in to see you but Marion has a bit of a cold right now and she's afraid to take her out. Also it's been quite chilly this week. April in Edmonton—what can you say?"

There was no response and Claire soldiered on bravely. "Marisa, I'd like to help you in any way I can. I can't take Tia's place, of course, but there must be *something* I can do?" Again there was no response.

Claire looked around the room and spied a heap of clothing in an open hamper in the corner. "Could I take those clothes home and wash them for you? I know how particular you are about your clothing!" This time Claire *did* see a slight glint of a smile. "I think you'd like me to do that, wouldn't you, Marisa?" she said, and headed towards the hamper to inspect its contents.

But just then she heard a dog barking and growling right outside the room, along with raised voices. Claire went to investigate and was shocked and surprised by what she saw. It appeared that a little boy about four had been so happy and excited to see a dog that he'd rushed over and grabbed him.

The sudden collision had knocked the woman holding onto the dog's leash to the floor and the dog was snarling angrily at the boy while the woman held on grimly to the leash. Seconds later, Claire realized that the woman was Hilda, Bill's cousin and the daughter of Marion, Bill's deceased aunt. The dog was Job—pronounced *Jobe*—after the man in the Bible story who lost everything of value in his life but still clung to his faith. This 'Job' was a Black Lab/Fox Terrier mix that Hilda had rescued from the SPCA shortly before his euthanasia date.

Just as Claire finished putting all this together in her mind, she observed that a nurse had her hand on the phone, preparing to call security. Claire acted quickly, grabbing the leash from Hilda's hand and leading the dog into Marisa's room. Hilda was unhurt and she scrambled to her feet and followed. The dog quieted immediately and pulled on his leash so he could stand beside Hilda. Claire relinquished the leash to her just as the nurse barged into the room with the Security Guard.

"You can't have that dog here!" the nurse declared firmly. "Get him out of here immediately!"

"He's a *therapy* dog," Hilda declared just as firmly. "I brought him here to see Marisa. She has a dog at home and maybe she will relate to him. Job has helped me a lot and I am sure he could help her." Hilda let go of the leash in her agitation and Job moved to the side of Marisa's bed where her hand was dragging out of the covers. He began licking it. Miraculously, Marisa slowly raised her hand and started stiffly stroking his head. "See! I *told* you he would be good for her!" Hilda gloated.

The security guard rolled his eyes. "Do you need me further, Inga?" he asked, addressing the nurse.

"I guess not," she replied. "I think I can handle it from here."

The guard left then without a word to the rest of them and the nurse turned to Hilda and stated imperiously, "He can stay for ten minutes but then he will have to leave. He cannot return unless you make arrangements in advance and either bring in a therapy dog registration certificate or a note from Marisa's doctor giving his approval." And with that, she flounced out.

Hilda glared after her but Claire said to her in a low voice, "Let's just focus on Marisa right now and later maybe we can go over to Tia's place together for a visit and tell her what happened." Hilda nodded but said nothing.

For the few minutes remaining to them, they just stood back quietly and watched as Job alternately licked Marisa's hand and pushed his head against it so she would stroke it. "He's an amazing dog," Hilda said proudly. "He has more empathy than most people—and a heck of a lot more than me!"

"You're right!" Claire said, not too politically. She picked up the clothes then and stuffed them into the extra bag she'd found at the bottom of the hamper. "I'll check with Tia on any suggestions she has for how you would want these washed, Marisa, and I'll see you tomorrow morning early before I go to work." And with that, Claire, Hilda and Job left.

"What were you doing at the hospital?" Tia asked Hilda, once they'd all arrived at her home in their separate cars and were sitting down with the promised tea and apple cake. Because her visit with Marisa had been cut so short, Claire had some time to spend with Tia.

"I was looking for something to do," said Hilda, "and I watched this documentary on TV about therapy animals. Job has been very helpful to me and I thought maybe he could help others. Amanda called me the other day and she mentioned that your mother had had a stroke and had recently been moved to the St. Jerome Extended Care Hospital. I thought maybe Job and I could visit her and it might help some."

"That was very thoughtful of you and I really appreciate it, Hilda," Tia said. After a pause, she added, "But I do think therapy dogs have to be registered. Have you looked into that yet?"

Hilda just blinked and looked dully at Claire and Tia. They both saw the hooded, shut-down look come over her eyes, a look they had seen so often since Hilda's mother, Marion, and Hilda's husband, Gary, had been killed.

"We could help you with that maybe," Claire said, looking meaningfully at Tia. Tia and her new husband, Jimmy, actually owed a bigger debt to Hilda for all the care and concern that Marion had shown to Jimmy's sister, Mavis, when Mavis had lived in an institution in Calgary. They had even named their baby Marion after her—her and Tia's mother—Marion Marisa Elves.

"I'll do some checking tomorrow when the baby has her nap," Tia added. "And I'll go next door and ask Amanda to check around on the net. She's good at that. Also, a friend of mine mentioned therapy dogs a while ago. I'll call her and phone you tomorrow night to tell you what I find out."

Hilda just nodded her head curtly, but neither Claire nor Tia were offended. They knew that Hilda was not really okay. She had not been okay since the murders.

Chapter 3: The Roommate

The next morning Claire was at the hospital by 8:15 for a quick visit with Marisa and to drop off her freshly washed and carefully folded clothing. That had been more work than Claire had expected. She had dutifully asked for Tia's input and it had been given in minute detail. Claire decided she wouldn't ask again!

After gently opening the door, Claire quietly entered Marisa's room, not wanting to awaken her if she were asleep. But then she backed up quickly and banged into the wall. There was a woman in the second bed and she was snoring noisily. The wall collision roused both women and the stranger started yelling. "Aah, aah ... nurse!"

The door opened suddenly and Claire retreated to Marisa's bedside, bracing herself for a scolding. But the care provider barely glanced at her before addressing the other woman. "Good morning, Mrs. Kravitz. What do you want?"

"I need to use the bathroom!"

"Not yet. You need to wait your turn. We're helping somebody else right now."

"But I need to go *now*!"

"That's what the diaper is for. Just *use* it." And with that, the attendant backed out of the room without another glance at anyone.

The woman began to moan loudly and soon an unpleasant smell filled the room. Claire glanced at Marisa and saw the look of despair on her face. Suddenly, Claire felt overwhelmed. She kissed Marisa softly on the cheek and explained that she had to get to work.

As Claire left the hospital, she was suffused in alternating waves of anger and guilt. She couldn't stand to see Marisa in that situation but she also couldn't bear to stay there any longer and witness it. *There has to be a way* was the mantra that hummed away incessantly at the back of her head all day as she worked first with Roscoe on some articulation issues, and later with Bill on some of his social barriers.

Roscoe spent three evenings a week at *The Three Musketeers,* serving as Maître d'. He greeted people when they arrived, checked for their names on the reservation list and then led them to their assigned tables. There were several pitfalls for him with this process. Roscoe's opening statement was, "Welcome to The Three Musketeers!" But when Roscoe said this, no matter how hard he tried, it came out, "Wehcuh oo Uh Fwee Musteer!"—and that was on a *good* day.

Even to get this much out of Roscoe had taken a lot of patient training on Claire's part. At the beginning, the best he could do was, "Wh-e-eh uh fwee mus," stated in a very flat tone. And he sometimes reverted to that form still at the end of an evening when he was tired. His articulation problems had nothing to do with a lack of understanding. He knew perfectly well what he was supposed to say. It was just that he had great difficulty guiding his normal sized tongue into the right position in his mouth because of his undersized jaw, a genetic anomaly shared by all individuals with Down Syndrome.

Claire *knew* this and that was why she persisted, working with him patiently until he could almost be understood most of the time. But this arduous process was only possible because of Roscoe's personality. He was by nature gentle, patient and trusting—possessed of a quiet dignity and a clear sense of his own worth as a person. But still, there were limits to what this process could do. So Claire had been developing a contingency plan.

When Roscoe just could not manage this phrase because he was tired or worried about something or not feeling well, Claire counseled him to fall back on one of his biggest strengths—his warm, charming smile—and to simply say, "Welcome to Roscoe's". When Roscoe said it, of course, it came out as, "Wehcum to Wosco," but most patrons were able to make the translation. As Claire worked with him on this phrase, she regretted once more that his Japanese parents had chosen a name beginning with r, impossible for individuals with Down syndrome to articulate clearly. *Why couldn't he have been born Chinese instead of Japanese?* she asked herself irritably. *They stay well away from* r*'s.*

The reason diners at the restaurant could make the connection to 'Roscoe's' was because Claire had arranged for 'Roscoe's Restaurant' to be printed right on the front door, just below the larger sign announcing it as, 'The Three Musketeers, or '3 人の銃兵,' the name in Japanese. This change had been made despite the aesthetic objections of Claire's architect husband, Dan, who had designed the restaurant door and interior—and the moral objections of Roscoe himself.

Dan's qualms had to do with the overall motif he'd developed for the restaurant. Claire's requested addition introduced a jarring, discordant note. Claire dealt with his concern by allowing the second name to be four inches below the official restaurant name, off-centered to the right, and in smaller letters and a different font.

Roscoe's objections had to do with not wanting to take the focus away from '*The Three Musketeers,*' the name he himself had chosen in recognition of his close relationship with Bill and Mavis. On an earlier group trip to Mexico, Claire and Tia had taken to referring to the three of them in this way.

Claire explained that it was legally *Roscoe's* restaurant. That was why he didn't have his parent's names or his uncle's name or his brothers' names on it either. Finally, Roscoe consulted with Bill and Mavis, and—receiving no clear negative from them, or *any* clear answer for that matter—agreed.

Chapter 4: Bill Takes on the Dining Room

That afternoon it was time to shadow Bill at the restaurant. Normally, he only worked there mornings back in the kitchen in a relatively private and quiet environment. There he happily peeled carrots, potatoes and other vegetables. Recently, he had begun cutting them as well, following a very specific training regimen that Claire had devised for him. But now she was hoping to introduce him to a different challenge.

Of the three individuals who lived together in the house across from Tia and Jimmy, Bill was by far the most volatile. And, as a result, finding a meaningful role for him in Roscoe's restaurant had been the biggest challenge that Claire had faced to date. The level of stimulation around Bill had to be strictly controlled while Roscoe was both social and socially skilled to a reasonable extent. That was why Roscoe, who was very interested—in fact, overly interested—in food, was out front. And Bill, who had very little interest in food and did not even seem to like it that much, was back in the kitchen.

But Claire was thinking of the future when perhaps the restaurant might not be there or at least not under their control, and Bill would need to have other skills in his repertoire in order to fit into the world. And she was also thinking of the present. The restaurant *was* making a profit at this point, but the margin was relatively thin and one never knew when new competitors might move into the area and thin it out so much that the restaurant could no longer remain open.

Several issues were contributing to this thin margin—staffing for one. Then there was the day/evening split. The restaurant did well on the three evenings a week it remained open to serve its Japanese cuisine prepared by Japanese master chef, Satou Botan, assisted by Roscoe's Uncle Daisuke. Roscoe helped out as Maître d,' supported when necessary by one of the young Japanese servers.

But the daytime clientele was a different matter. It consisted largely of retired folk coming in to visit with their friends and play cards. They tended to nurse their coffees for hours and to splurge on a donut about once a week.

Then there was the staffing issue. The servers were often careless, unreliable and lazy, and tended to quit at the drop of a hat if something better came along. Claire couldn't blame them really. The only way waiters could make anything approaching a decent wage was if they pulled in substantial tips. And day tipping was poor.

Mulling over these issues one night in bed just before sleep claimed her, Claire came up with a possible solution. And if it worked, it could be a win-win situation for both Bill and the restaurant. Bill had none of the characteristics of the restaurant's daytime servers. In fact, in many ways he was their opposite. He was reliable, enjoyed working and was obsessively precise and cautious. And he did not care at all about tips since he had no clear concept of money.

But the downside was his frequent anxiety attacks that, when unchecked, led to some spectacular meltdowns. His anxiety manifested itself primarily around unfamiliar people when he didn't understand what was expected of him or around unfamiliar situations where he didn't know what to expect. Busboys cleared empty tables and checked with occupied tables to see what dishes could be taken away. The restaurant badly needed a reliable busboy and that was the position Claire had in mind for Bill but she would have to approach it in stages with him.

Claire considered the situation carefully. The restaurant was never full in the afternoons and, in fact, was sometimes almost empty. She laid off the most recently hired and, as it happened, the laziest of the three daytime wait staff, explaining there were too few patrons to warrant the current staffing level. Then she asked one of the two remaining servers to take over Bill's kitchen work two mornings a week so he could work out front on two of the days when the restaurant was not open in the evening. She also asked the wait staff to space out the clients in order to make the room look more occupied to passers-by. The servers tended to seat the customers right next to each other to save themselves extra steps, a tactic that had always annoyed Claire, sensitive to people's need for privacy and breathing space.

Claire's next step was to place a portable sign near the door during day hours that read: "Please place any dishes no longer needed on an empty nearby table for pick-up. This will help us to keep your costs down." Of course, this was not the real reason for the dish moving. It was to minimize Bill's interaction with clients so he wouldn't get overly stressed.

Claire had been talking to Bill about his possible new job for a while and predictably he was nervous and resistant to a proposed change in his life. But Claire assured him that they would begin by practicing when the restaurant was closed. That way it would be quiet and they would be alone in the front. The next day, a Tuesday, she asked the daytime wait staff not to pick up any more dishes from the tables after 3 p.m. Then at four, she arrived with Bill.

Bill didn't look too happy to be there, out front and exposed, and Claire understood why he felt that way. Also, she knew that he couldn't stand scraping noises or tolerate getting his hands dirty. Order and harmony were everything to him. Therefore, he was never going to be willing or able to just stack dirty dishes higgledy-piggledy on top of other dishes with food on them and carry them back to the kitchen that way, which is what the other front workers did.

Claire got out two long, green aprons purchased from Ikea and beautifully embroidered across their front pockets, one with Bill's name and one with hers. This was Tia's handiwork and Claire had gasped when she'd seen them, awed by their smooth, professional look.

"How did you *do* that, Tia?" she asked.

"I removed the pockets first. Then I used a twin needle to do the double stitching in the two shades of green and I adjusted the feed-dogs so I could sew freehand with the embroidery stitch on my Janome machine. And then I sewed them back on. It wasn't all that hard."

Claire had looked admiringly at her friend and then thought, with a sudden pang, that Tia had likely acquired that skill from Marisa, now lying there inert in the hospital.

Claire put her apron on and wrapped the long straps around hers waist, tying them in front. Bill looked at her approvingly and then put his apron on, slowly and elaborately tying the straps in front in a perfect bow. Tying things was one of Bill's favorite activities.

Next, Claire handed him a pair of industrial grade, extra long rubber gloves that slid on easily because of the thickness of the rubber. Fortuitously, they'd been available in a green color just slightly darker than the aprons. Bill put them on and then walked over to look at himself in the mirror just inside the front door. He touched his hand to his head and Claire groaned. She knew what was coming.

"Hat! Where my hat?" Bill asked.

Although she'd been hoping it would not happen, Claire had purchased online a 3-pack of "one-size fits all" sailor hats and now she placed one carefully on his head. Bill looked at himself in the mirror and grinned. The obvious solution might have been to point out that the other front restaurant staff did not wear hats, but Claire had known that that line would not work. Bill was clearly thinking of

Daisuke and Satou Botan back in the kitchen with their fancy hats, not of the attire of the front restaurant staff—and certainly he had no concept of the busboy's place in the overall restaurant hierarchy. He obviously thought his new position required a hat and she knew better than to try to argue with him. That tactic just didn't work with people like Bill.

Bill was clearly satisfied with his appearance but now he looked inquiringly at Claire and pointed at her head. She shook it vehemently. "No, Bill, I can't wear a hat because my hair will get all messed up and I won't be able to fix it afterwards." Bill nodded, accepting this decision better than some might have expected. Everybody who knew Claire, including Bill, came to realize sooner or later that she was particularly self-conscious and unhappy with her hair.

Claire's next step was to role model for Bill how to bus a table, her style. She picked up a tray and laid it down on a table with dirty dishes on it. The tray held three items: an empty metal pie plate, an oblong plastic dish and a soft, silicone spatula. The spatula was an odd choice but Claire knew that if she asked Bill to scrape the excess food off with a knife, the way the other servers did when necessary that he would make jarring, scraping noises that would likely upset both himself and the customers.

All this time, Claire didn't say a word. It was easy to confuse and overwhelm Bill with words and it was generally more effective and less stressful for him to just show him what to do. She slid the remains of some beef stew into the pie plate with the aid of the spatula but now the spatula had gobs of stew on it. Bill looked at it nervously. The next plate held some left over salad and scooping that into the pie plate actually helped to clean the spatula a little. But when she used it to brush a few cake crumbs off the desert plates, some of the remaining stew stains transferred to them and she saw Bill tense up. Hastily, she stacked the cups on top of the plates, picked up the remaining cutlery and headed for the kitchen with Bill at her heels.

"Now it is your turn, Bill," Claire said brightly when they returned to the dining room.

Bill looked at her and nodded his head. The first dirty dish he picked up held some left over spaghetti. He awkwardly cleaned this into the pie plate with the spatula, having yet to master the necessary twist of his wrist to do it smoothly. But then Bill continued to clean the dish, not stopping until there was absolutely nothing left on it. It took a lot of convincing and a good week of practice for Bill to accept that he needed to leave something for the dishwasher to do and that he couldn't stand there laboriously cleaning all the food stains away because it would make the clients nervous. But gradually Bill and Claire reached a reasonable compromise.

On his first day of actual work, clearing dishes in the restaurant, Bill was proceeding along quite effectively, if rather slowly, when a female patron in the midst of an animated discussion swept her hand across the table for emphasis and knocked a full cup of coffee onto the floor. Bill jumped and screamed and then stood there frozen. Claire, who was shadowing him, hastily grabbed a mop from the kitchen and started sopping up the spill.

"You pick up the broken pieces, Bill," she told him. "But be careful so you don't cut yourself!"

Bill knelt down awkwardly and slowly and meticulously picked up every piece, stacking them neatly inside an empty soup bowl on the tray of dirty dishes he'd been collecting. This activity required care, focus and precision and by playing to his strengths in these areas, Claire knew she could help him regain control of the situation. Another of the servers brought out a clean mop to do the final cleanup and Claire and Bill retired to the kitchen to take care of the sopping mop and discard the broken crockery. But Bill was still shaking a little and Claire suggested that they sit down together at a small table tucked into a quiet corner of the kitchen.

"Things happen, Bill. You need to understand that," Claire said soothingly. "That is what I want you to learn. But right now I need you to fold these napkins," and Claire handed him a laundry basket full of them, still warm from the dryer. She knew that the best way to calm Bill was to set him up with a simple, repetitive task that he could feel complete control over. Once he was engaged in that and looking calmer, she left him so she could quickly bus the remaining tables herself.

Chapter 5: Claire Refines Her Laundry Techniques

Over the next two weeks, Claire eased into a regular routine of visiting Marisa on Monday, Wednesday and Friday, either before work or after, depending on the demands of her day. She continued to faithfully do Marisa's laundry but the items that needed to be ironed she took to Tia. Claire did not iron!

Tia examined the items—mostly blouses—closely before ironing them, and when she found the residues of stains, she worked on them further. Since she'd asked Claire to wash all Marisa's outer clothing in cold water and hang them to dry, further stain removal when necessary was often possible.

Claire marveled at Tia's collection of stain removers, her knowledge of fabrics and of the effects of different stains on different materials. "You really should be a professor of home economics if such a job category still exists," she told Tia one day. Tia just laughed ruefully and resorted to one of Claire's aphorisms. "Ah. If wishes were horses, beggars could ride."

"What about that book you were planning to write and the course you were designing?" Claire asked.

"Well," Tia responded, pointing her arm in the general direction of the now sleeping Marion, "I obviously got side-tracked, didn't I?"

"But you have so much to say. You're going to pick it up again, aren't you?"

"I hope so," Tia replied. "But right now any extra time I have is going to have to be spent helping my mother."

"I know," Claire responded. "But just don't forget about it. What you know about house cleaning and laundry is amazing and needs to be shared!" Tia smiled in response but it was a sad smile.

As is often the case when one does something kind for others, there's a reward. In Claire's case, the extra laundry duty combined with Tia's tutoring gave her ways to get some of the more troublesome stains out of Jessie's clothing. Jessie tried to help when she was fed even though she had no hand coordination. Even after years of training and even when Claire resorted to heavy hand over hand support, Jessie could not bring a spoon to her mouth without jerking her arm spasmodically. This resulted in a mess and caused her to choke—and when her hands were untied the mess was even greater and the choking was worse, a couple of times so severe that it had resulted in aspiration pneumonia.

Claire knew that aspiration pneumonia was the biggest killer of individuals as severely disabled as Jessie and had received special permission to implement a "restrictive procedure." Padded cuffs had been attached to Jessie's wheelchair tray and were used to restrain her hands while she was being fed. However, she still frequently choked and spit food out, getting it on her clothes as well as the table, the floor and often her assistant's clothing as well. This she did in spite of her impressive collection of snugly fitting terry cloth and plastic bibs that she wore at every meal, drink or tooth brushing session. Sometimes Claire wondered if Jessie was doing it on purpose because she resented having her hands tied! Even though she couldn't communicate a word by mouth or by sign, Jessie and Claire had a real relationship and it often seemed to Claire that Jessie was trying to tell her things.

Claire did Marisa's laundry at the Co-op during the day. At first, she found all this new learning in stain removal that she was acquiring and implementing very satisfying, but after a while, removing the same stains over and over just became another tedious chore. One day, after working away at one too many grape juice stains, she stomped over to Tia's house and vented. "You know how good you are at stain removal? Well, I know an even better way. Don't get the darn stains on in the first place!"

"And how do you propose to get that to happen?" Tia asked mildly. Claire didn't answer directly but instead asked a question of her own. "Why do you suppose that three-year-olds, who spend chunks of their day at pre-school or day care finger painting, don't come home all stained up?"

"Smocks," Tia replied.

"So why then are Marisa and the others at the hospital who have to be fed not wearing smocks when they eat?"

"'Normalization'? Gee, Claire, I thought you of all people would *know* that!"

"Of *course,* I know it—only I call it *pseudo-normalization.*"

"What do you mean?"

"Kids need smocks to protect themselves just like people need capes when they get their hair cut. The care providers are just anxious to get the job done. They're not interested in protecting the clothes because the clothes are the laundry's problem, not theirs."

"You're harsh!"

"No, I'm not. You haven't been there as much as I have."

"Well, what do you propose?"

"I propose that if people have to be fed like that, they be covered with plastic capes to protect their clothing so at least they don't have to sit around all day with food stains on them. That's far more degrading and de-normalizing in my opinion than wearing a smock. And furthermore, the time and energy spent on washing out food stains that need not be there—and in the process wearing out the clothes prematurely—could be spent on quality interactions. *That's what normalization comes down to in my books!*"

"But they do put those giant bibs on some of them!"

"Yeah!" Claire snorted. "Nice and loose at the neck so the food can trickle down, but carefully avoiding the sleeves so they can get all spotted up!" Tia realized that Claire was on her soapbox again and the best thing to do was to not respond. But Claire went home that day thinking that this was a subject requiring further thought.

Claire continued to visit Marisa, bringing her back the fresh clothing that was already beginning to show signs of wear with the frequent washing and the extra scrubbing and treating necessary to remove stains. Claire, never overly fond of housework, saw this as the perfect example of diminishing returns. But she had promised to do this and she would keep her promise. And the laundry was not the only irritation.

Almost every time Claire opened the door to Marisa's room for a visit, she was confronted by the angry, screaming, bed-ridden Mrs. Kravitz who just assumed Claire was a nurse no matter how many times she explained otherwise.

"Nurse, I have to go to the bathroom. I have to go *now!*"

It was becoming clear that this was not always the case and that Mrs. Kravitz was not functioning normally. But when she did soil herself, her tears and obvious mortification were real—real and overwhelmingly sad for anyone witnessing this display with any degree of human compassion.

Up to this point, only the noise level had appeared to be bothering Marisa but gradually she was becoming more aware, and as her awareness increased, so did her own agitation when these incidents occurred. Claire reported all this to Tia and urged her to insist that Marisa's room be changed. Tia was loath to take little Marion to the hospital and only visited on weekends or evenings when Jimmy was home to care for the baby. Of course, no administrators were available at those times and Linda, the receptionist on duty on the weekends, was not at all helpful—unlike Alma, the friendly receptionist who worked during the week. Linda just kept telling Tia to come back during the week and didn't appear interested in hearing about her scheduling problems. Tia tried phoning during the week, but all she was told was that there were no other rooms available and none expected in the near future.

Chapter 6: A Problem Is Solved?

It was 8:10 on a Wednesday morning, two months after Marisa's stroke, and Claire opened the door gently, hoping Mrs. Kravitz was still asleep and that Marisa was awake enough so they could have a whispered—albeit one-sided––conversation.

She glanced furtively at Mrs. Kravitz's side of the room, listening for the telltale snores, but there were none. Claire braced herself for the usual onslaught but there was nothing. She tiptoed over and noted that the woman's eyes were partly open. Yet she didn't seem to be registering Claire's presence.

Claire glanced back at Marisa who appeared, by the sound of her soft, even breathing, to be still sleeping. She reached over and touched Mrs. Kravitz lightly on the wrist and said timidly, "Good morning, Mrs. Kravitz?" It came out as a question and when there was no response, Claire wrapped her fingers around the lady's wrist to check for a pulse. She found none. Claire looked at her face then and could see that her lips were blue. She hadn't noticed them at first because the morning light was only beginning to creep through the curtains. She stood back and thought.

Claire was not one to panic and she considered her options. Carefully, she opened the blinds part way so she could see more clearly. Regarding Mrs. Kravitz again, she noticed a tiny feather poking out of her nose. Claire quickly grabbed her cell phone and took several pictures at different angles. She gently pulled back the woman's nightgown to check for bruising or choke marks but there were none. Then she did the only thing she could do. She rang the bell to summon the nurse. But the nurse didn't come.

Obviously, they were used to Mrs. Kravitz ringing the bell, as she had some use of her right arm, and they were in the habit of ignoring it. Claire headed for the nursing station. She was able to find a nurse who quickly came and confirmed Claire's suspicion. Mrs. Kravitz was dead. The nurse called for a doctor to sign the death certificate. A Dr. Gerhardt arrived and within one minute he had confirmed the death and instructed the nurse to call for a gurney to transport Mrs. Kravitz to the hospital morgue.

Claire, who was still hanging around despite having been asked several times to leave, objected. "There was a feather in her nose which means she may have been smothered. I'm not convinced this was a natural death."

The doctor gave her a look which could only be translated as, "you are presumptuous and interfering," and proceeded to ignore her.

"I have pictures," she said. Claire had anticipated his resistance and had already sent them to her computer. "And I'm calling Inspector McCoy, a homicide detective at the police station. You're interfering with a crime scene. The doctor stood back—temporarily intimidated—and Claire quickly made the call. McCoy had just arrived in his office and wasn't happy to be interrupted before settling into his morning routine. However, he listened with as much patience as he could manage.

"What position is she in and has she been moved or handled?" he asked Claire, once she'd finished describing the situation.

"She's on her back the way I found her. I only took her pulse and pulled back her nightgown at the neck to check for choke marks. There were none. The doctor and nurse only took her pulse as far as I can tell."

"Let me talk to the doctor," McCoy snarled. Claire handed Dr. Gerhardt her phone and, of course, couldn't hear what was said. However, after completing the call, he instructed the nurse to find another room for Marisa and to close off the room until the police arrived.

Marisa was awake by this time and looking confused and upset by all the talking and the number of people in the room. An orderly came in to wheel her out and Claire saw, with a thrill, that Marisa seemed to be looking at her as if to say, "Aren't you coming?" Claire was really torn. She so wanted to share this moment of awareness with Marisa but she knew that McCoy or his sergeant was on the way.

"I'm coming, Marisa," she called to her, as Marisa was wheeled through the door. I won't be long".

The doctor turned to her. "You can leave now."

"Inspector McCoy will want me to be here when he arrives"

"We're bringing in a new patient. You can't be here."

"You can't do that! This is a crime scene. It needs to be protected."

Dr. Gerhardt turned to a male nurse and jerked his finger at Claire. The nurse touched his beeper and took Claire by the elbow but, just as they reached the door, McCoy entered. He scanned the room, flashed his badge and said, in his meanest, flattest voice while pointing at Claire, "She stays. Everybody else out! This is a crime scene."

Just then, an orderly arrived at the door, presumably to assist with the expulsion of Claire. Almost simultaneously, another orderly came down the hall, wheeling a gurney that he attempted to negotiate through the door. "Out!" McCoy snapped, pushing the gurney back.

Once the gurney was back out into the hallway, he closed the door to the room, now empty except for himself, and Claire. He walked to the bed where Mrs. Kravitz lay and gently moved her nightgown away from her neck, but he moved it even further down than Claire had, revealing her shoulders and upper arms. Pulling a small but professional quality camera from a kit he'd carried with him, McCoy quickly snapped several close-ups of her face, neck, upper chest and upper arms. Then he checked the time and wrote it down in his little notebook.

Turning to Claire, McCoy explained, "The crime scene team is on the way but the sooner we get the visuals the better."

Claire pulled out her phone and showed him the pictures she'd taken. "I didn't get the arms. I didn't want to disturb the body that much. And my cell phone has fairly low resolution."

McCoy studied them. "You didn't get the time, I suppose?"

"Yes," she replied, pulling out her own notebook, "8:14." McCoy looked at her appreciatively but said nothing. Claire had the courage to go on. "When I turned the lights on I saw that her lips were blue. I checked her pulse and there was none. Her arms were in a different position," she said and looked at him questioningly.

"Show me," he said, and Claire gently arranged them in the angelic, sleeping position that she'd first observed.

"Hmmm," he said, checking her wrists. "Thumbprint here," he pointed out, and began taking more pictures.

"The doctor removed the feather from her nose. I asked him not to but he ignored me. I got a picture, though," and Claire flicked to the first picture she'd taken on her phone.

McCoy checked the woman's pillow carefully. "Yellow stain here. We need to find out if she takes eye drops at night."

"What about saliva?"

"People drool in their sleep, particularly *old* people," he replied, with a hint of the old condescension in his voice.

"Oh, yes," Claire said meekly, and just then the crime scene team arrived. McCoy brought them up to date and then took Claire by the elbow with surprising gentleness. She had begun to shake—delayed reaction.

"Let's do the interview in the cafeteria," he suggested, and Claire nodded her head gratefully.

The interview proceeded along the lines Claire had come to expect. Why was she there and why so early? What exactly had she done when she came in the room? Why did she turn the lights on? What was the first sign that made her suspicious? How long had she known the deceased? What was she like? Why did Claire think someone would want to murder her?

Claire answered as best she could and then asked her own question. "You *do* think she was murdered, then?"

"Yes. The signs are subtle but they are consistent with smothering. If you hadn't been there to tell us how you found her, if you hadn't seen the feather and taken a picture and if you hadn't called when you did—and if I hadn't trusted your instincts and come out—murder would never have been suspected."

Claire didn't know what to say. Their relationship had been complicated, to say the least, fraught with enmity and condescension on both sides. But by this point, they had shared a lot of crime scenes, too many not to know each other's strengths and weaknesses. Claire could have called McCoy's sergeant, Michael Crombie. He was always more open-minded and respectful towards her, and much easier to talk to. But she'd detected a level of arrogance and chauvinism in Dr. Gerhardt that made her think she needed McCoy. Beside, timing had been critical. Sergeant Crombie might have needed to consult with McCoy first, anyway, and that would have meant a further delay.

Chapter 7: Claire Gets Busy

After the interview, Claire searched out Marisa's new room, feeling very guilty because so much time had passed. Marisa was sleeping again and Claire arranged the few clean clothes she'd been carrying with her in the storage space provided. She noted that the rest of Marisa's clothing had not yet been moved, but assumed that the nursing staff would take care of that.

Claire left then and headed for work, her mind roiling with conflicting thoughts and feelings. She felt a pleasant sense of vindication. McCoy had trusted her enough to come out. That in itself was a miracle. And then he'd found her to be right. Mrs. Kravitz *had* been murdered. *But why and by whom?* Claire asked herself.

As she parked in the driveway of Roscoe's home, Claire mulled over the questions McCoy had asked her. She looked longingly across the street at Tia's house and thought how wonderful it would be to go over there now and discuss the situation. But Claire had her duties. Roscoe was waiting and she was already more than an hour late. Fortunately, he was quite capable of managing on his own for periods of time since there had been no opportunity to arrange relief staff. Claire had only taken the time to make a quick call to him explaining that she'd be late, and asking him to take a shower and get dressed nicely for a visit later.

When Claire greeted Roscoe, he recognized immediately that something had happened? "Wha wong, Claih?"

Claire looked at him and weighed her response. But she didn't know how to respond—or for that matter how not to respond and just go on with the day as if nothing had happened. After the trauma he'd been through a couple of years ago, she wanted to shelter him from another murder. But he *knew* she was not herself and she could see that he was anxious about her.

"I'm going to phone Tia and see if we can visit her. You look very nice by the way. I like that shirt on you and you combed your hair very well this morning." She noted it was still wet from his shower and asked, "You didn't try to blow dry your hair this morning like I showed you?"

"Too *hahd,*" Roscoe replied sheepishly, shrugging his shoulders.

"That's okay, Roscoe," Claire replied soothingly. "It's not all that important in the larger scheme of things," and even as she said it Claire realized how true that was. She gave him a quick hug and picked up her phone to call Tia.

"Marion just went down for her nap so this is a *great* time, Claire. Come on over!" Tia responded. And after a moment she went on, "Something's happened, hasn't it?"

Claire gulped. Tia's sisterly-like empathy came close to unraveling her. "We'll see you in a minute," she replied with a catch in her voice, and hung up the phone.

Roscoe and Claire sat down on the sofa and Tia sat on a chair across from them in her family room, her baby monitor close at hand. They could hear Mozart's Eine Kleine Nacht Musik (Serenade No. 13) playing quietly over it and Claire raised her eyebrows.

"Marion likes to go to sleep listening to Mozart serenades and she seems to have a particular fondness for that one," Tia commented with a note of pride in her voice. Then she motioned towards the basket of still warm and fragrant smelling oatmeal-raisin muffins sitting on the table in front of them. A pot of coffee sat beside them on a tray with three cups, cream and sugar. Roscoe hadn't been able to avoid picking up the coffee habit after all the time he'd spent in the restaurant.

Tia and Roscoe were both looking at Claire, waiting for her to begin. She gulped and reached over to take Roscoe's hand. She told them both then what had happened. Roscoe jerked his hand away and turned to her with uncustomary fierceness. "*Why*? Why people always huhting people?"

"I don't know, Roscoe, but I intend to find out. Marisa is there and I want her to be safe." Tia was notably silent and Claire looked at her now. She was crying.

Claire gasped. "Oh, Tia! I'm so *sorry*! I was so worried about Roscoe I wasn't even thinking about you, about Marisa being there with a murderer around."

"I feel so helpless!" Tia exclaimed, openly weeping now. "Marion is still not sucking well and she's way too thin. I don't dare cart her around and risk her getting an infection or even getting over-stressed."

"I know *one* thing!" Claire said. "The best way to keep Marisa safe is to make it very clear to everyone there that there are a lot of people looking out for her. With your permission, I'm going to arrange a roster of regular visitors. If she has visitors once or twice every day, whoever did this is much less likely to pick on her, assuming this murder wasn't specifically directed at Mrs. Kravitz for some reason."

"*I hep. I visit!*" Roscoe interjected.

Claire regarded him for a moment, running various calculations through her mind before she answered him. Then she replied, "Yes, Roscoe. We're really going to need you in on this, but I'm just going to have to get the okay from your parents first. You have something the rest of us don't have—flexibility in your schedule. I can arrange for DATS [1] (Edmonton's *Disabled Adults Transportation System*) to take you there and pick you up a couple of mornings a week. You can take some homework with you to keep you occupied when Marisa is asleep."

Roscoe groaned in response but Claire was not listening. Even as she'd been saying this, her mind was racing. It was part of her dignity theory for people with disabilities that ways should be found for them to make meaningful contributions, i.e. something other than shredding paper under the bored gaze of an overseer. This was perfect—and Roscoe had even volunteered!

Claire glanced at Tia hoping to share the moment but Tia was wrapped up in her own thoughts and had obviously not engaged in the same inner dialogue. Claire reached over and grabbed her hand. "We won't let anything happen to Marisa, Tia. But as soon as she's recovered enough to function a little better and we're sure she's medically stable, we're going to get her out of that place!"

"How?" Tia wailed. "Dad can't manage—and I can't help."

"I have a plan—but I'm not talking about it yet!" Tia looked at Claire hopefully but Claire said nothing more, and shortly after, she and Roscoe departed.

Chapter 8: What Next?

After she finished her work with Roscoe for the day, Claire headed back to the hospital. Marisa had been moved to a room on the east side of the unit where at least she had a view of the front of the building with its green lawn and tall spruce trees rather than the parking lot.

"Hi, Marisa. How do you like your new room?" Claire asked in a cheerful voice. Marisa looked at her and smiled wanly. She'd been showing a few more signs of awareness over the past week or so.

"You have a better view here," Claire continued, going over to the bed and giving Marisa a brief hug. Marisa raised her left arm and tightened it around Claire ever so slightly. *I must tell Tia!* Claire thought exultantly. This was the first sign of independent movement she'd seen from Marisa since the dog incident. *Maybe all the fuss this morning and the move shocked her and woke her up a bit? Who knows how the brain works!* Claire thought.

Claire checked through Marisa's drawers and closet to make sure all her clothing and personal items had been moved. They appeared to be all there but when she looked for Marisa's fancy tortoise shell brush so she could brush her hair, Claire couldn't find it. She turned and said, "Marisa, I'm going back to your old room to search for your brush. It's not here!" And with that she left.

When Claire cracked open the door to Marisa's old room, she could see that one of the housekeeping staff was already busy getting the room ready for new patients. Claire checked the drawers and the bathroom but couldn't find the brush and when she asked the cleaner, she said she hadn't seen it. Claire next went to the nursing station to report that the brush hadn't been moved with Marisa's things and to ask if it had been found and brought there for safe keeping, but the answer was no.

"It was on the table beside her bed when I left this morning," Claire stated. "Somebody must have seen it and put it somewhere?"

"One of the patients may have walked in and taken it. They do that sometimes." Claire nodded and walked away. There was nothing more she could do. She'd been told the same thing when the beautiful mohair cardigan she'd brought as a gift for Marisa and wrapped around her shoulders one afternoon before leaving, had mysteriously disappeared.

Thieves! Murderers and thieves! We have to get Marisa out of here! Claire fumed to herself as she walked back to Marisa's room. But when she got there she found that Marisa was asleep again and felt doubly frustrated. She'd missed the brief moment when they might have been able to communicate because of a hairbrush!

Claire drove home totally preoccupied and mumbling to herself, having to be extra cautious to avoid a driving error. The last time she'd felt this frustrated was when Bill had been accused of murder and incarcerated. She'd sworn to herself then that she would vindicate him and she felt the same sense of determination now. She would get Marisa out of this situation one way or another.

Claire visited Marisa again the following afternoon after work, determined to search further for the brush. Alma, the receptionist, greeted her on the way in and Claire decided to check with her about the brush and ask if she had any ideas about how to track it down.

"Marisa brought that brush with her from Italy as part of her trousseau," she explained to Alma. "At this point, it's an antique and undoubtedly worth a fair penny, but quite apart from that it has huge sentimental value for her."—*if she ever recovers from her stroke,* Claire added to herself.

"I've been here a long time," Alma commented, "and a number of people have come to me with complaints about lost items. I've been told to tell them that they were either lost in the laundry or taken by another patient."

"It doesn't sound like you believe that yourself?"

The receptionist leaned in closer to Claire and said in a low voice, "I don't know, but I suspect it's probably one of the staff members. It just seems to happen too often. And if it were really one or more of the patients, you'd expect it to turn up in their clothes or for one of the care providers to notice because everything is labeled. But please don't quote me on that. I could get into trouble!"

Claire just smiled and nodded her head. "Thank you!" she whispered. "At least you were willing to talk to me, unlike the nurses I've asked." Claire pulled out a poster she'd prepared with a picture of the brush scanned into it. She had taken the picture because the brush was so unusual and beautiful. The poster included contact information and the offer of a small reward. "Could I hang this up out here somewhere?"

"Unfortunately, no. Not without getting an okay from administration. And I don't think they'll agree to that. Others have tried to hang up posters of lost items in the past and been turned down. The official excuse is that the hospital doesn't want to give families the impression that there is thievery going on here when it's likely just a patient who is perhaps dementing and no longer has a clear sense of property rights."

Claire looked frustrated and Alma peered closely at the poster and took a picture of it with her own cell phone. She said, again in a whisper, "I'll keep my eyes out for it whenever I visit a staff washroom. That's where it's most likely to be brought out in the open. If I do run across it, I'll contact you. I find these thefts pretty disgusting. We're all supposed to be here to *help* people, not *steal* from them!"

Claire nodded her head appreciatively. "Thanks, Alma. It is nice to know that at least one person here is willing to help me find the brush. I certainly didn't get that impression from the nurses on Marisa's unit."

Alma said nothing more but the look on her face suggested that she knew what Claire was talking about. Claire left then and a few minutes later, she was in Marisa's room and was surprised to see that the other bed was now occupied.

"Hell-o!" the pleasant-looking woman in it sang out in lilting tones.

"Oh, hi," Claire said with minimal enthusiasm. She was not in the mood to socialize. "I'm just here to visit Marisa and drop off some of her clothes. My name is Claire—and you are?"

"Ella. Ella Burbidge. I fell down and broke my left hip and the doc put a pin in and now I can't walk," she babbled. "I have to stay in this bed until they can get me a wheelchair where I can keep my leg out straight. It's very boring. Do you play cards?"

Claire, who was an overly serious person with little skill in greasing social wheels just looked at her. "No time," she said, and walked over to Marisa's bed. Marisa had her eyes partially open and Claire smiled down at her. "Do you remember moving this morning, Marisa?" There was no response. "I brought you this to keep your special things in," she said, pointing to the small cedar box with a locking mechanism on top that she was carrying. "I'm going to put your jewelry and your watch in it for safe keeping and, whenever you want something out of it, I'll bring back the key and open it. Is *that* okay?" Marisa just looked at her.

"Tia knows," Claire went on, "and she said it was a good idea."

Claire busied herself collecting Marisa's jewelry and watch that had just been thrown in a drawer during the move. She didn't know if everything was there but took a picture of the collection to show Tia and Alberto. Tia's father drove into Edmonton to stay with Tia and Jimmy and visit Marisa quite often but still remained alone in Wetaskiwin much of the time. He just found these visits very upsetting since Marisa often didn't seem to recognize him.

When Alberto had brought Marisa's things up to the hospital, he'd collected whatever he knew was important to her so she would feel more at home. Tia hadn't been able to be there to put in a cautionary word because some of those items definitely should not have been brought to the hospital.

Over the next two weeks, Claire continued to come in regularly. She noticed that the staff members were rather cool to her, probably because of the fuss she'd made over the brush, but Alma continued to give her a big smile whenever she passed the reception desk.

On a couple of occasions, Claire noted that Inspector McCoy and Sergeant Crombie were interviewing various staff and visitors, and the second time she had the opportunity to speak to Sergeant Crombie alone. He was much more likely to share information with her than McCoy. "How is it going, Michael," she asked. Claire and her entire group of fellow amateur detectives, particularly Tia and Tia's 70-something neighbor, Amanda, and Claire's similarly-aged Aunt Gus, were on a first name basis with Sergeant Crombie at this point—except when Inspector McCoy was around.

"We haven't been able to unearth a single suspect and Donald is about ready to give up."

"But you *do* still think it was a murder, don't you?"

"Well, the markings on the body were consistent with suffocation but the marks were pretty faint. It *is* possible they were caused by normal handling."

"What about the way the arms were positioned? I *know* they were posed. *Nobody* sleeps like that!"

"Well, like I said, we're pretty much at a dead end. We'll probably wrap it up tomorrow."

Claire was fuming when she left the hospital and she stopped at Tia's house on the way home even though it was suppertime and Jimmy was back from work. She could tell by the look on his face when he answered the door that he was not happy to see her. "I need to talk to Tia for a few minutes," Claire said assertively.

"What happened?" Tia asked. She was behind Jimmy now, holding baby Marion in her arms.

"I talked to Michael this afternoon. They were both at the hospital. He says they haven't found anything and they're going to wrap up the investigation tomorrow. McCoy's thinking now that maybe it wasn't murder!"

"But the signs!"

"I know. But Michael says there's nothing more they can do."

"What about the roster?" Claire and Tia between them had lined up more than a dozen people to take turns visiting Marisa. Roscoe was going twice a week and his parents, Uncle Daisuke and two nephews, Gerald and Thomas, were also helping out. Alberto had rounded up three of their mutual friends who still lived in the city and could drive, and Jimmy and Tia's 11-year old son, Mario, were going as often as possible. Mario was even being allowed to take the bus by himself on occasion. Claire's Aunt Gus and her new husband were going every Thursday morning and Tia's neighbor, Amanda, went a couple of times a week.

"I think we should keep it up for the time being. And I don't think we should tell anybody else about them stopping the investigation. Do you agree?" Claire asked Tia.

"Yes!" Tia said gratefully.

Chapter 9: It Happens Again!

It was a Thursday when Claire heard this news and she was too busy that Friday for her usual visit. She didn't return to the hospital again until Monday at 7:30 a.m. Claire needed to get an early start on the day as she and Roscoe had special plans. She continued to notice that, since the time she had indirectly accused them of theft, staff members no longer greeted her as warmly as they had previously. But now there seemed to be a real edge of hostility in some of the glances directed her way. It was apparent from a few of the comments she overheard that they were becoming irritated with the excessive number of visitors Marisa was receiving. *And they've probably figured out that I had something to do with it,* Claire thought.

Claire smiled at the unit clerk briefly as she passed the nursing desk and proceeded down the hallway to Marisa's room, opening the door gently as it was still very early. She noted right away that Marisa was asleep but heard no noise from the other side of the room even though a dim overhead light was on. Claire got an ominous feeling and crossed over immediately to Mrs. Burbidge's bed.

She touched her hand which seemed quite cool, and whispered, "Hello, Ella. Are you awake?" There was no response. This time Claire didn't hesitate. She turned on the bedside lamp and stared at Ella's face. Again, the blue lips! She turned on the second light and took Ella's pulse. No pulse. Claire quickly took pictures, noted the time and called Inspector McCoy. He informed her that he and Sergeant Crombie would be there in 15 to 20 minutes. Then she pulled back Ella's nightgown the way she'd seen

McCoy do it on the previous occasions, and took a number of pictures. Only then did she press the bedside bell to call the nurse.

A nurse arrived very quickly, almost before Claire had time to hastily rearrange Ella's nightgown and store her cell phone. "What are you doing here so early?" she snapped, obviously assuming that Ella was still asleep. "And what do you want?"

"This woman is dead," Claire said coldly. "And the police are on their way."

"Who gave *you* the authority to call the *police*?" the nurse, whose name was Beatrice according to her nametag, demanded. Meanwhile she was busy taking Ella's pulse.

"The God of Common Sense," Claire responded drily. "And don't touch the body!" Inspector McCoy gets very upset when that happens.

Beatrice pushed her alarm beeper and a second nurse came running. "Call the doctor," Beatrice told her. "We have another death."

As it happened, it was the same doctor, Dr. Gerhardt, who arrived a few minutes later to take over the situation. But, less than 30 seconds after that, Crombie and McCoy walked through the door. "Stand back!" McCoy snarled. "Michael, check the body!"

Sergeant Crombie went through the same ritual as Claire had done previously and then reported, "There are no unusual bruises or pressure marks on the upper body. Do you want me to look further?"

"Check high on her neck, just behind her right ear," Claire suggested.

McCoy glared at Claire but Crombie did as she suggested.

"There's a puncture mark here, sir!"

The inspector came over to the body and examined it carefully. "We'll need a complete tox screen. Tell the team to take blood as soon as they get here!"

"Shouldn't we wait for the medical examiner?"

"No. Some of these poisons disappear rapidly from the system. I'll square it with him when he gets here. My understanding is that he's out on another case and will be a while." McCoy turned to the medical staff in the room and said, "Everybody out! This is a crime scene now. Move that woman!" He was pointing at Marisa.

Marisa was wide awake now and looking at McCoy. Claire was trying to calm her and to phone the home at the same time to tell them that once again she would be delayed. She turned to Inspector McCoy then and said pleadingly, "Please don't move Marisa again. All this action has made her more alert. We're trying so hard to bring her back to us and moving her again would only disorient her. We can pull the curtain if you wish."

McCoy looked at Marisa. Then he walked over to her bed. "Ma'am, are we disturbing you? Would you like to be someplace quieter?" Claire looked at him in surprise, not expecting such a gentle response. But McCoy was remembering his own mother and wishing he'd been more considerate of her during her last days. In one way or another he'd been trying to atone for that ever since her death.

Marisa looked directly at McCoy with eyes wide open. She spoke then in a whispery voice, "Let Claire help y-o-o..." Her voice faded away then and her eyes closed. Marisa appeared to be asleep again. McCoy touched her cheek gently and turned to Claire. "She can stay," he said in a gruff voice. "And so can you. But *don't* interfere!"

Claire just shook her head but didn't speak. She had tears in her eyes and a huge lump in her throat. Marisa had said something intelligible, something that made sense. Marisa was still there! McCoy pulled the curtain around the bed as he left. "You can pull it back if it gets too stuffy in here," he said.

Claire sat inert for several minutes, mechanically stroking Marisa's hair and processing what she'd just experienced. She'd seen a whole different side to McCoy just now—and Marisa had spoken! *You just can't write people off,* she said to herself. *You never really know what's going on in somebody else's mind.* Then she pulled the curtain back.

Just at that moment, the medical examiner came in and, after talking to McCoy briefly, he quickly checked the body, took a second blood sample, and had the remains of Ella Burbidge removed to his lab for immediate autopsy. He too expressed concern about capturing the evidence of any residual toxins in the blood before they dissipated.

As the body was being transferred to a gurney for removal, the crime scene team came in and began their work. Then Inspector McCoy and the medical examiner left to confer privately. McCoy had witnessed the scene between Marisa and Claire and must have realized that Claire didn't want to leave Marisa alone. He didn't require her to come away for an interview, but simply asked that she write down exactly what had happened that morning while it was still fresh in her mind and come down to the station later to make her formal report. Claire nodded her head and smiled at him gratefully, marveling at his newfound sensitivity.

As she sat on the bed, still holding Marisa's hand, Claire noted the two crime scene techs kibitzing as they went along. Perhaps, Claire thought generously, they needed to do that in order to cope emotionally with gruesome crime scenes day after day.

They lavishly sprayed a special solution on the walls and floor and bed frame and bedding and then checked the entire area over with a light. Nothing happened. Presumably they were looking for blood stains although there was no reason in this case to assume that they'd find any. Then they did what seemed to Claire to be a rather cursory inspection of the mattress, and then the floor area and took a large number of pictures. Within twenty minutes, they were gone.

A cleaner came in shortly after to sanitize that side of the room in preparation for the next patient. She worked alone and Claire had the impression she liked it that way, as the young woman seemed very serious. Claire wondered idly about her for something to focus on other than sitting there, holding Marisa's hand while she slept. *She must be in her early twenties*, Claire speculated. *And she works very quickly and efficiently. Tia would be impressed. I wonder how she ended up being a cleaner?*

As Claire let her thoughts run, she was suddenly aware that the girl's rhythm had been broken. She was staring at the far back corner where the end of the bed had been before she moved it out. Just as she reached out for something, Claire realized what was happening and jumped off her chair. "Don't touch that, whatever it is!" she whispered urgently.

Claire crossed the room quickly to see what the girl was looking at. She took a couple of pictures with her cell phone. Then she grabbed a Kleenex and reached for the object wedged into the back corner. It was a clear plastic cap.

"How did *that* get there?" the girl asked. "I mopped this room yesterday and, unlike some, I work right into the corners. It wasn't there at ten to four yesterday afternoon. I can swear to that."

"How do you know the exact time?" Claire asked.

"It was the last room I did before the end of my shift."

"It looks like the cap from a hypodermic needle," Claire whispered, looking over her shoulder. She didn't want any nurse coming in now to interfere.

The girl looked at it more closely. "It looks about the size that goes on a 25 gauge needle, the kind used for subcutaneous injections like if you get a flu inoculation or a pain killer, for example."

"How do you know that?" Claire asked, surprised. "It can hardly be part of your cleaning job."

"I'm just doing this job because I have no money to go to school and because I really want to be a nurse. This is the closest I can get to it right now. Sometimes the nurses tell me things and one of them who came back and upgraded even gave me some of her old books. A lot of things have changed, of course, but the basics are still the same, like needle size, for example. I study those books sometimes when I'm off work."

Claire looked at her with admiration and then asked her, "When are you through with your shift for today?"

"I work 10 to 6 on Mondays. I start late because I always work Sundays. This was my first job of the day. Why?"

Claire did a quick mental calculation involving care provision for Jessie and then asked, "Would you care to come out to dinner with me? I'd like to get to know you better. I admire you."

The girl shook her head wistfully. I can't spend the money. I'm saving every penny for school. If I start indulging myself like that I'll *never* get there."

"No! You don't understand. I meant as my treat."

"Why?" the girl asked simply.

Claire looked towards the door. Jimmy and Mario had just entered and she waved at them. She turned and whispered to the girl, "When's your break?"

"I'm due for one just as soon as I put this mop and pail away. I'm finished in this room now."

"Can you meet me in the visitors' waiting room down the hall in five minutes? I'll explain then."

The girl looked thoughtful for a moment and then nodded her head.

"Good!" Claire whispered, touched her lightly on the shoulder and then moved over to Marisa's bed to greet Tia's husband and son and explain what had happened.

"What was *that* all about?" Jimmy asked.

"Marisa's roommate was murdered some time early this morning. The girl was just asking me if I'd heard anything further about it. That's why I'm still here. I didn't want to leave Marisa alone. But now that *you're* here I guess I can go."

"Wait a minute!" Jimmy demanded. "Exactly what happened?"

Claire explained as quickly as she could and then rushed off to the visitors' waiting room, fearing that the girl would be long gone since more than ten minutes had passed. And she didn't even know her name.

The girl was just leaving as Claire arrived. Claire gently pushed her back into the room and closed the door behind them. "I only have five minutes left on my break," was all she said.

"I'll talk fast," Claire promised, "but you have to promise not to repeat what I tell you."

The girl nodded her head and Claire explained her relationship to Marisa and her concern that something would happen to her next. "I need someone on-site to help figure out who the murderer is," she blurted out in conclusion.

The girl looked at her blankly. "You haven't even told me you name—and my break time is up."

"Claire. Claire Burke. And you are?"

"Hazel Burnham."

"How do you get home from work?"

"The bus."

"Meet me at Tim Horton's on the corner after work. I will be there waiting for you at 6. That's when your shift ends today, right? We can go for supper and I'll drive you home afterwards. I know things about this situation and I'll tell you more then. Please? I need your help."

Hazel hesitated, studying Claire carefully. It had been an odd, quirky exchange but somehow she must have found it reasonable. Finally, she replied, "I'll be there about five or ten after."

"Great! See you then," and Claire turned on her heel and left, mulling over the situation as she headed quickly to her car. The last thing she wanted to do was to start any gossip and have it eventually get back to McCoy when he was just beginning to trust her. But she needed this girl on her side. Her instincts told her that Hazel could be trusted to be discrete but she'd have to get further assurance from her before sharing.

Claire arrived at the Co-op to discover that Roscoe had yet to take his shower. While he was doing that, she phoned Dan. Jessie's assistant would be there until eight that night and her supper was already prepared. There was just the small matter of Dan's evening meal. Claire suggested that he make himself an omelet.

"What are you up to *this* time, Claire?" Dan growled.

"Somebody else was murdered here this morning," she blurted out. "Marisa's new roommate. I'm going out with someone I hope will function as an inside person for us, one of the cleaners here."

Dan was predictably shocked and said nothing for a minute. And when he did speak it was to urge her to be careful. "It could be *anyone* there. How do you know it's not her?"

Claire thought about that for a moment. *Hazel had seemed to know a lot about needles.* But no! Her instincts told her that Hazel was okay, that she wouldn't hurt anybody and she could be trusted. "I have to go. I'll see you about eight or a little later, Dan," and she hung up the phone.

Hazel was already waiting for her when Claire cruised into the Tim Horton's lot at 6:05. Claire opened the front passenger door for her and pushed some stray pop cans and chip bags into the back seat. As Claire pulled out of the lot, she asked Hazel, "Do you have any food preferences or allergies?"

Hazel responded, "I haven't visited enough restaurants to form any preferences and in my house we couldn't *afford* to have 'allergies'!"

"Some allergies are *real*," Claire retorted, picking up on Hazel's tone.

"I suppose so," Hazel replied wearily. Claire suddenly remembered that Hazel had been working all day and since she apparently did a thorough job she must be tired.

"We'll just go to my favorite restaurant, Red Lobster, if that's okay with you. Do you like sea food?"

"I haven't tried it much but I'm game."

"There's just one thing, though," Claire added.

"*What?*" Hazel asked suspiciously.

"We need to drop this needle cap off at the police station. It's right on the way. If there's any residue, it needs to be analyzed as soon as possible."

"Fine. I'll wait for you in the car."

"It's not that simple. Inspector McCoy will want a statement, but it should be quick. The two of us there together will be able to verify each other's story." Claire had phoned ahead and knew that McCoy would be there, working late.

Hazel didn't look happy. If Claire had known the whole story she would have known that Hazel had already had plenty of negative experience with the police in her short life. Her mother got lonely from time to time and she seemed to attract the wrong kind of man.

"It'll be fine," Claire added pleadingly. "And it really *is* important. When you're working on a case you never know in advance what will be the critical piece of the puzzle."

Finally, Hazel agreed. Fortunately, McCoy was in a good mood when they arrived. He took the needle cap from Claire by holding onto the Kleenex in which it was wrapped so as not to touch it. Hazel was able to quickly and clearly explain how she'd found it and how Claire had intervened to prevent her from picking it up. Claire showed him the pictures she'd taken of its location and told him how the tech team had seemed to concentrate on the walls and the mattress but never really pulled the bed out to examine the floor. By her tone, McCoy could probably tell that she hadn't been impressed but Claire didn't say as much.

"I'll get this cap to the print team for analysis in the morning—and I'll also check with the nursing station to see if Mrs. Burbidge was given any prescribed injections between yesterday afternoon and this morning."

Claire nodded her head in approval and in less than 15 minutes they were out of there.

Chapter 10: The Group Gains a New Ally

Claire studied the menu avidly. Menus held a peculiar power for her. They made her feel safe and in control and hopeful and expansive—as if her world were bigger than it seemed to be at times. After careful thought, she ordered the dueling lobster tails and turned to Hazel, but Hazel just looked at her in confusion.

"I have no *idea*!" she said.

"Do you want to have what I'm having?" and Claire pointed to the menu picture.

"No! Those things look ugly."

"How about shrimp? Do you like shrimp?"

"Maybe?" Hazel nodded her head tentatively.

"Okay. I know just what to order for you and you're going to *love* it!" Claire turned to the server and placed an order for Coconut Shrimp.

Over glasses of Stella Artois—Claire had convinced Hazel to try her favorite beer—they began exchanging information about themselves. Claire avoided mentioning Jessie because she wanted to keep the conversation as focused as possible.

"The reason I'm at the hospital so much these days is because Marisa is the mother of my best friend who just had a baby a couple of months ago and isn't very mobile yet. Tia worries constantly about her mother but she trusts that when I go there I'll tell her exactly how she is. She also signed permission for me to talk to the doctor about Marisa so I do that whenever I manage to see him when I visit. Marisa had a stroke just two weeks after Tia's baby was born and she still isn't really awake much. And this is the *second* time that her roommate has been murdered. Marisa was on the west side before, and they moved her after the first incident."

"Oh! That's *terrible*," Hazel said predictably. Claire nodded her head grimly.

"Yes. Tia is worried sick about her mother being there on her own."

"Is there anything I can do?" Hazel asked.

This was the response Claire had been waiting for and she launched into a brief rendition of the past detective work she and her allies had done. "Having somebody on the inside is *very* important, and the fact that you have a known interest in nursing and can therefore ask questions about certain nursing procedures without raising suspicions will, I suspect, be key to solving these crimes—assuming you're willing."

Hazel's eyes were sparkling and she nodded her head enthusiastically. It occurred to Claire that as dutiful as she was about cleaning, Hazel was probably also very bored by it. She thought it might be time to tell her about Tia. "My friend is a cleaner *par excellence*. She's even writing a book about cleaning techniques and developing a course on proper cleaning. You *have* to meet her."

Hazel looked intrigued and Claire went on. "In two of our murder cases, Tia actually arranged to get hired as a cleaner at the crime sites—once at a restaurant and once at a hospital. What she was able to find out just talking to other cleaners and keeping her eyes open made it possible for us to solve those cases."

"*I* could do that!" Hazel said, her eyes gleaming.

"It can be dangerous," Claire said, and she told her frankly about a couple of things that had happened.

"I want to try," Hazel said simply.

"Well, if you're sure. I really don't think we'll get anywhere without your help. Inspector McCoy was just going to give up on the first case when the second one happened."

"You told me before that there was something you'd be willing to share about this current case," Hazel reminded Claire.

"Oka-a-y," Claire said slowly. "But you have to promise not to repeat it to anyone. It could jeopardize the whole operation, and if Inspector McCoy ever found out I told you he'd never trust me with any information again."

"I promise," Hazel said soberly. And Claire believed her. She had already noted the cautious way Hazel talked and how she avoided talking about other people.

"There was a puncture mark behind Ella Burbidge's left ear. That's why the cap you found could be an important clue. It might have a tiny drop of medication on it or a partial fingerprint."

"O-o-h," Hazel breathed. "It could be a nurse then, or even a doctor. In fact, it wouldn't be a good idea for *anyone* to know. You can get everything over the Internet these days including needles and instructions on how to inject them. In fact, did you know that even if you inject just air it can kill someone? That's why nurses always do that little 'bloop' thing with the needle before they poke it in."

"Yes, I know that. But I'm hoping in this case they did use something else so maybe we can identify it and track it to its source."

Their meals had arrived, and Hazel and Claire carried on their conversation between bites. At first, Hazel kept commenting about how tasty her shrimp were, but then she started to slow down and her facial expression changed. "My mouth is beginning to feel all crawly," she said to Claire. "They're not still alive, are they?"

Claire stopped eating and looked at Hazel, concerned. But even as she looked, she saw red splotches breaking out on Hazel's face and noticed that she was beginning to have difficulty breathing. Hazel's symptoms went from mild discomfort to life-threatening anaphylaxis in what seemed like seconds, and for a moment Claire just gaped at her horrified. Then she stood up and yelled at the nearest waiter. "Call an ambulance! Emergency!"

Claire looked hopelessly at her big, overloaded purse and then rushed to an empty table nearby. She searched frantically through the contents but could not find her epi-pen. Finally, she remembered that she'd stored it in the inside zipper compartment for easy access. She rushed to open the zipper and it jammed. Desperately, she grabbed a nearby table knife and managed to carve a jagged hole in the soft cloth of the zipper compartment. She felt inside and grabbed the epi-pen.

Back at the table, people were crowding around Hazel and giving advice to each other in panicked voices. Claire pushed them roughly aside and gaped at Hazel. Her lips were a deep purple, almost black. With clumsy fingers, Claire ripped the cap off the epi-pen needle and jammed it straight into Hazel's leg, right through her trousers. Then, with strength she didn't know she had, Claire flipped Hazel onto the floor and began administering CPR.

Just a couple of minutes later, two ambulance attendants barreled through the door and over to Claire's table where they took over but Hazel was already beginning to come around. Claire told them what she'd done and they returned to their vehicle to bring in a gurney. "I'll follow you in my car," Claire said, "so I can explain what happened." Meanwhile, she was struggling to get everything back in her purse, and hoping she'd find enough bills to pay for their meals without having to wait for her credit card to clear. But one of the onlookers was the manager and he just waved her away. "Go quickly. Don't lose them. Forget the bill!"

Claire nodded her head in thanks and ran out the door, but the ambulance was already racing ahead with its siren on. Claire did her best to follow, hoping no police car was around. She'd forgotten to ask the paramedics which hospital they were taking Hazel to and was very afraid she'd lose them. At that moment, she couldn't even remember Hazel's last name.

Soon it became clear that the ambulance was heading for the Grey Nuns Hospital in the southeast part of Edmonton and Claire relaxed a little. Even though she lagged behind, Claire was able to identify the ambulance when she pulled up in the emergency entrance at the Grey Nuns and she caught up with the attendants.

Hazel was rushed right into one of the examining cubicles and Claire followed boldly after. A young male resident came in almost immediately and asked Claire for details. Claire explained what Hazel had eaten and what had happened. "Hazel didn't mention any allergies," Claire told the doctor, "but she wasn't very familiar with shellfish and I'm not even sure if coconut might be an allergen for her, as well as the shrimp."

The doctor checked Hazel over and determined that she'd better remain in the hospital for a few hours just to be sure, but if she continued to recover at this rate she could go home after that. He recommended that Hazel carry an epi-pen from now on and left.

Claire, seeing that Hazel was now resting comfortably and was being closely monitored by the nursing staff, left the cubicle and the building so she could park her car properly and call her husband.

"*Why* do these things always happen to you?" was his unsympathetic response. Claire was shaking at this point with a delayed reaction and could have used a little warmth from him. She told him so and Dan apologized, told her not to worry about Jessie and advised her to get some hot tea with sugar in it.

Claire went to the cafeteria and managed to scrounge a leftover apple fritter to go with her tea. She thought it was thoroughly justified under the circumstances, particularly since she'd only managed to enjoy a couple of bites of her delicious lobster before she had to abandon it.

The resident returned to check on Hazel at 1:15 in the morning and pronounced that she had recovered enough to leave safely. He reiterated that Hazel should purchase an epi-pen and suggested a source. Then he left. By 1:30, they were in Claire's car.

On the way to her house, Hazel told Claire that despite what had happened she was still interested in participating in the project.

"I'm at the hospital visiting Marisa three times a week," Claire told her, "but I don't think we should talk or even acknowledge each other when I'm there. For you to stay safe and have a chance of rooting out any useful information you'll have to stay deep under cover." Claire enjoyed the way those words rolled off her tongue and suddenly realized that she was no longer feeling bored and depressed. *Sick!* But she went on speaking to Hazel anyway.

"Also, we need to make very sure that Inspector McCoy doesn't catch on to what you're trying to do. That would make him really angry and he'd immediately blow your cover." *A-a-h, it feels so good to be back in the game,* Claire thought.

"Don't worry, Claire," Hazel said dryly. "I'm used to being regarded as a nonentity and I can play that role very well." But after a moment, she asked, "How will I contact you then?"

Claire rooted in the side pocket of her purse and handed Hazel a card. "Here. You can reach me at my cell number before five or call me at home any time after that before ten. But don't call from work just in case you're overheard. When are your days off?"

"Wednesday and Saturday."

"Can I pick you up Wednesday afternoon so we can go over to Tia's house and you can meet her?"

"Yes, I can manage that but I'll meet you at the 7-11 on the corner. It's just as well if my mother doesn't know what we're up to. She gets worried and upset very easily."

"Okay, I'll meet you there at two on Wednesday if that's okay for you."

Hazel agreed and they rode in silence the short distance remaining to her house. Home was a run-down rental bungalow in South East Edmonton. Hazel had told her that she lived there with her mother and three younger siblings and took the bus to work each day—an hour and 20 minute bus and light rail transit (LRT) ride, involving two transfers.

Hazel looked ashamed as she followed Claire's gaze to take in the rundown and depressing exterior with its peeling paint and sagging screen door, and the front yard with its patchy brown grass and the rusting children's tricycle and deflated rubber ball laying half across the broken wooden walk. *I wonder what it's like to live that way?* Claire asked herself. *At least, I should be grateful for some things.*

Claire said goodnight quickly and left, suddenly longing to be back in her own home with Dan and Jessie. It was admittedly a little dusty in places, but basically in order, and the yard was well maintained by Dan. Claire thought about him then and wondered how she could have managed with Jessie with a different kind of husband or no husband at all. Jessie and Dan had a very special relationship and he was more motherly towards her than Claire was in some ways.

Chapter 11: A Beginner Lesson in Snooping

On Wednesday afternoon, Claire picked Hazel up as agreed and they headed for Tia's home. Claire noted that Hazel had taken pains to dress up a bit. She had on black pants and a cheerful blue and black striped sweater. At a glance, Claire could see that both these items were discount store brands, and on her feet Hazel wore inexpensive blue tennis shoes in an apparent effort to match her sweater. Hazel's short brown hair had been carefully curled and she had on lipstick and blue eye shadow, the latter seeming a little out of place for a casual afternoon visit. Claire felt a pang of sorrow for this girl who obviously had so little and so little to look forward to unless her circumstances changed drastically.

Tia was ready for them and they sat down with Earl Grey tea and some fresh apple cake still warm from the oven. Soon Hazel and Tia were talking animatedly about their shared interest in efficient house cleaning techniques. It wasn't long before Tia was asking her if she'd be interested in taking on a couple of house cleaning jobs in the Mill Woods area, not too far from her home. Tia had such a reputation as a first class cleaner that people were still being referred to her

"I finish at the hospital at four every day of the week except Monday. If they were willing for me to do it after that, I certainly could. Otherwise, if there were at least a couple of them I could take the bus on Wednesdays or Saturdays, but the bus ride is so long it wouldn't be worth it for just one."

"I'll call them and see what I can work out," Tia said. She was pretty sure, by her past experience, that each of these contacts would have at least one other friend longing to have a good, reliable house cleaner.

Claire and Tia talked to Hazel at length then about the murders.

"You'll need to think about a possible motive before doing anything else," Tia warned. "What, for example, do these two women have in common? That's always a good place to start."

"Mrs. Kravitz was very disagreeable in my opinion," Claire commented.

"Yes, I remember her," Hazel responded. "One day when I was cleaning her room she kept demanding that I take her to the bathroom. When I explained that that wasn't my job, she called me a 'lazy tramp.' No, I wouldn't say she was a nice person. But that Mrs. Burbidge seemed quite different. When I was in there one day, she offered me a chocolate from a box she'd just received from a visitor and she called me 'dear'."

"She *was* a pleasant soul," Claire said thoughtfully, "although she was frequently pestering the nurses about needing to go to the bathroom, too, albeit in a much nicer way than Mrs. Kravitz."

"Surely, *that* can't be what they had in common," Tia interjected.

Hazel was looking impatient and now asked, "Well, where do I start?"

Claire shook her head to clear away some niggling thoughts and responded, "Start slow. Don't say anything about this to anybody. Don't even act interested. Talk about yourself and your future plans when you're socializing with others there. And if McCoy comes around and recognizes you, just be polite and brief. Don't let on about the needle mark to anybody unless he brings it up—and I don't think he will. He's pretty discreet and businesslike when he gets going on a case from what I've seen."

Tia jumped in then. "What worked for me when I was cleaning in an institutional setting was to share my interest in cleaning techniques. I found someone there who felt like I did about cleaning and she became a very important ally in finding the killer."

"Actually, she inadvertently led us towards a giant red herring and that mistake almost cost you your life as I recall," Claire replied drily.

"I *still* don't know what I'm supposed to do," Hazel said.

Claire vaguely registered Hazel's complaining tone and then she got a certain look in her eyes.

"*What?*" Tia demanded.

"Complaining! The only thing we know that those two women had in common was that they complained a lot, demanding attention. Just keep you nose to the ground and your ears open. That's what I advise. Listen in on gossip in the coffee room and act interested in other staff and be nice to them, maybe bring in some homemade cookies to share so they'll be more inclined to talk to you. Find out if anybody else is a complainer"

Hazel just looked at her, and Claire remembered her situation. "Okay, I'll meet you before your shift one day and bring the cookies. Just tell them you baked them. I'll bring the recipe and you can review it in advance in case they ask questions." Claire looked thoughtful for a moment and then went on, "They need to be interesting, unusual cookies so you can get a conversation started."

Tia smiled when she saw the sparkle in Claire's eyes. It had been missing for a while now. Claire and Hazel agreed on a time to meet for the cookie exchange and then it was time for Claire to drive her back to the 7-11. Before leaving, Claire pulled out a Winners bag with an insulated lunch container in it. She'd noticed that Hazel used a plastic store bag for her lunch. "Tell your mother you bought this so she won't be wondering where you went," Claire said.

Hazel began to object with her usual poor but proud line to the effect that she didn't want charity, but Tia cut her short. "This has nothing to do with charity and everything to do with remaining under cover. It's merely the cost of doing business, and our business is to find the killer, preferably before he or she chooses a third victim."

Claire and Hazel left then with Claire elaborating on strategy and necessary precautionary measures all the long way back to the far south-east end of Mill Woods. It was agreed that Hazel would now temper her cleaning zeal by taking regular coffee breaks so she could interact with the other staff. On Monday, the day Hazel didn't start work until ten, Claire would meet her at the bus stop a couple of blocks from the hospital at quarter to ten with the cookies and after that, Hazel was to call her as soon as she had something positive to report—but only when she was well away from the hospital and any possible listening ears.

On the following Monday, Claire delivered the cookies--an intriguing combination of walnuts, dried cranberries, coconut, rolled oats and whole wheat flour, sweetened with Stevia and with unsweetened apple sauce substituted for part of the fat so they were not only healthy but guilt free.

"*That* should get somebody talking," Claire told her. But she had to wait until Thursday to hear back from Hazel. She was just about to leave work when her cell phone rang.

"Hi, it's me," Hazel said cryptically.

"Where are you?"

"Phone booth, 7-11 near my house."

"We gotta get you a burner phone. People will get suspicious if they see you there too often," Claire responded, unconsciously lapsing into jargon picked up from *CSI* programs on TV. "Should we meet somewhere?"

"No. I'll be quick. The cookies worked. One of the other cleaners started talking to me about them. I said I'd get her a copy of the recipe and she asked me where I lived. I told her, and she only lives about ten blocks from me. She asked how I got to work and when she found out I took the bus, she offered to carpool with me when we have the same shifts and we mostly both work eight to four except Mondays."

"But what did she have to say about the murders?" Claire asked impatiently.

"The topic didn't come up and I didn't ask. I thought it was better to wait to get to know her better and let it arise naturally."

Claire sighed. She knew Tia would have approved of this approach. It was exactly her style. But not Claire's style. She would have barged right ahead—which was why she needed Tia for these investigations, she realized. And now Hazel.

"I'll phone you again if and when I get something worth reporting," Hazel added, and hung up the phone abruptly.

Claire held the dead phone in her hand and thought, *But I can't leave it all to her. She may or may not get something.* Across the street Tia was having exactly the same thought, but there was another matter even more pressing that she had to take care of first.

Chapter 12: Tia Faces the Truth

Tia's baby, Marion, was now 2 ½ months old. She was already reaching for things and curious about what was going on around her. Physically, she was within normal limits for height but near the bottom of her range for weight.

From the beginning, Marion had been a fussy eater and early on Tia had had to resort to supplementing her with some formula after breast-feeding. Marion seemed to have difficulty latching onto the breast and the effort tired her so that she tended to quit nursing before she was full. And then, after the bottle-feeding, she often regurgitated a larger amount than normal.

For months, Tia had been living with the unspoken fear that Marion had a genetic disorder that had plagued a branch of her mother's family in Italy and was transmitted through the female line. It involved a gradual neurological deterioration beginning with early signs of digestive discomfort and failure to gain weight.

Normally, Tia would have been able to talk to her mother about her concerns, but Marisa had had her stroke when Marion was just two weeks old. And Tia couldn't bring herself to share her fears with Jimmy. He was so happy with Marion, and with her and Mario, so grateful to finally have a loving wife and a family of his own. She just couldn't cast any shadow on his happiness so she'd suffered in silence.

Sometimes Tia had thought of sharing her fears about Marion's development with Claire, but again something stopped her. Perhaps Claire would get on her soapbox about normalization. Or maybe, with all the expertise and experience she'd acquired through living with Jessie and associating with other parents in similar situations, Claire would look closely at the baby and see something that Tia didn't want to see.

Tia felt that all she could do was to hover over Marion, rigidly adhere to her feeding schedule and never trust her with anyone, except Jimmy, for her occasional visits to see her mother in the hospital. She rarely took Marion out even for walks. Her pediatrician dismissed her fears, declaring that there was nothing wrong with the baby and refused to order any special tests except one for hypothyroidism that had just come back negative.

Finally, one evening, Jimmy had had enough of Tia's moroseness and compulsive concern over Marion and he demanded to know what was bothering her. Still she couldn't bring herself to tell him about the hereditary disorder and simply explained that Marion didn't seem to be eating as well as she should. "Then take her back to Dr. Carvel and insist that he do some tests to find out what the problem is."

"But he *won't*. I already asked."

"*Insist*! Do you want me to book off work and come with you?"

"No."

"I want you to phone tomorrow and make the appointment," Jimmy demanded, and then he retreated to the family room to see what was on the sports channel.

Mario had been listening to this conversation with concern and now he said, "Mom, do you think you should get a second opinion? You've always said that Dr. Carvel doesn't seem to take you seriously. Not all doctors are the same, you know."

"There's a shortage of pediatricians in Alberta. If I go to somebody else, he'll hear about it and then he might not be willing to see us anymore. Besides, you can't just phone up a doctor and go. They all have their protocols."

Mario just shook his head. "Jim-Dad is right. You're not yourself lately. You have to do something.*"*

The next morning when Marion had her nap, Tia phoned the doctor's office. But she was told that he was away on a two-week holiday and his new office partner, a Dr. Faron Yonge, was covering for him in his absence. Would she like to see him?

"Yes!" Tia gasped, amazed by this stroke of luck. And the very next day she was able to bring Marion in for a late afternoon appointment.

Dr. Yonge was an older man, originally from South Africa, who'd had a rich and varied experience in his field. He had spent considerable time in tropical countries, and listened carefully to Tia's concern about a possible hereditary blood disorder. He examined Marion closely, much more closely than her regular doctor had ever done, and then he turned to Tia and spoke gently.

"I will send you to the lab with a requisition for some blood work, but I really don't think that's the problem. I would expect to find some indication of swelling in her liver or spleen if there was a blood disorder or some sign of rattling in her lungs if she was having a big problem with reflux. What I *do* see is a fairly serious tongue-tie and that alone could explain why she's had so much difficulty with the breastfeeding. With your permission, I will clip the tie now. It will only take a minute and cause her minimal discomfort and bleeding. You should see improvement in a day or so."

Tia looked at him in amazement. "Why did Dr. Carvel not tell me this?"

"I can't answer that," Dr. Yonge said tersely, and Tia thought that his very terseness was itself a judgment.

Tia's own energy, sapped for months by overriding fears, came surging back. "Do you mean to tell me that all we've been struggling through for months with Marion might be due to nothing more than a simple tongue-tie?"

"It seems likely," the doctor replied. "It would explain her difficulty nursing, the frustration and anxiety that would then build up in her, her tendency to then drink the bottled milk too quickly with the result that she regurgitates afterwards, gets a stomach ache and is fussy."

Suddenly, Tia knew that what he said made sense and that her fears for something more ominous were very likely groundless. She felt as if a great weight had been lifted and she looked at him gratefully. Timidly, she asked, "Would you consider taking over as Marion's doctor?"

The look he gave her was difficult to read. She thought she saw compassion there as well as some anger over what had clearly been a case of medical incompetence but there was also a note of caution. Finally, he replied, "I am new to Edmonton. I came here for the final stage of my practice and am in semi-retirement. I only come in three days a week and I can't guarantee to be around until Marion graduates." He stopped then but when Tia said nothing he went on. "But if you are sure this is what you want, I can take her on as a patient."

"I'm quite sure," Tia said, and if Jimmy had been there he would have reveled in the note of quiet self-assurance in Tia's voice that had been missing for so long.

"May I do the tongue-clip now?"

"Please."

In what seemed like seconds, it was over. Marion cried for a moment and then closed her eyes and seemed to sleep. "Here is the requisition," Dr. Yonge said, handing it to her. "I want you to get the blood work done just to be sure. If you don't hear back in a week or so, you can assume that the results were negative and if you *do* hear back it may be some minor, easily correctible thing like mild anemia, so don't panic. It there is nothing, I would like to see Marion in a month for another check-up."

Tia gathered Marion up and left then with a spring in her step and a sense of lightness she hadn't felt for months. Despite the incision, Marion slept well that night and when she awoke at four in the morning for her regular breastfeeding, she latched on eagerly and sucked much more efficiently than usual. Tia was simultaneously thrilled and angry that such a simple solution could have saved them both so much grief.

The next day, when Marion had her mid-morning nap, Tia reached a decision. She was going to start taking Marion to the hospital. She also noted, looking idly through the community paper, that there was a local group of mothers of young babies that met twice a week. She was going to try that out as well. It was time to get their life back on track.

When Marion awoke from her nap, Tia nursed her, again with surprising success, and then readied her for a walk. She was feeling restless with a resurgence of her old energy. She looked critically at her house and realized that her usual high standards for house keeping had been sliding but that was not the priority right now. Rebuilding her life and expanding Marion's life were definitely more important goals.

At lunchtime, Tia phoned Claire and asked her if she and Roscoe would like to come over around 2:30 when Marion had her afternoon nap.

"That should work. It's Roscoe's day off from the restaurant and we were just going to go to the library but that can wait for another day. I'm sure Roscoe would much prefer a visit with you and Marion."

Tia got busy and made a brown sugar pound cake that she served with scoops of maple walnut ice cream. Roscoe silently looked at the cake and then at Claire after he finished his serving. "Okay, Roscoe. You may have a second piece—but no more ice cream."

"Okay, Claih." He grinned happily. "Yo cake is vewy *good*, Tia," he commented. "Tank you".

"You're very welcome, Roscoe," Tia said warmly. "I always appreciate your comments about my cooking. You are one of my best supporters."

Claire had been noticing the lift in Tia's voice, so absent in recent months. "Okay, Tia. What happened at your doctor appointment yesterday?" Tia told her the story then and shared the fear that had been haunting her for months.

"Oh, Tia! Why didn't you *tell* me? Marisa talked to me about that when you were pregnant."

"She *did? Why?*"

Claire looked sheepish. "I asked her if there were any hereditary concerns in your family because I heard that among Southern Italians there was a higher than expected incidence of pernicious anemia due in part to inbreeding and in part as an evolutionary defense against malaria. She mentioned that a number of individuals in one branch of her mother's family from Thessalonica had suffered from that, but explained that her mother's cousin had married a woman from a malaria-prone part of North Africa and that's where it had come from. It had nothing to do with your mother's immediate family."

"Well, I wish she'd explained all that to me. I only remember relatives talking about it when I was a child, but I didn't know how close the family connection was or anything more about it except that it was hereditary."

"You should have told somebody—me or Jimmy. You shouldn't have kept it in all this time and suffered so much."

"I know that now," Tia said, but just then Marion awoke and Tia went to her room to change her. When she brought her out, she nursed her, and Marion suckled easily and contentedly.

"Wow!" Claire said. "What a difference from the *last* time I saw you nursing her."

"I *know!*" Tia said. "I'm so angry with Dr. Carvel for missing the tongue tie. It's not as if I didn't tell him something was wrong every time I saw him."

"Don't be angry. You got even—you switched doctors. And look at the positive side. This way you found a *good* doctor."

"I know," Tia responded. "I *am* very grateful for that."

Meanwhile, Roscoe was staring at Marion but there was nothing salacious in his look and it didn't make Tia uncomfortable. Finally, he said, "Dat bootiful. I wish *I* had a wife and baby guhl."

"I know, Roscoe," Claire said softly, and she reached over and patted his shoulder awkwardly, knowing herself that it was a poor substitute for all he was missing in life.

"I have *girlfriend,* though," he said shyly.

"You *do?*" Tia and Claire asked together. *"Who?"*

"Her name Patty. She comes to westauwant evy Wednesday when I wohk theh. Some day I tell heh we go *out.*" Roscoe grinned when he said this.

Roscoe's remark was followed by a moment of silence as Tia and Claire took time to absorb it. Then Tia said rather weakly, "Well, we want to meet her sometime. Maybe you and Claire could bring her over here for coffee and cake. Would you like that?"

"Yes, that nice," Roscoe said politely. But he added, "And then we want to go out alone—on date."

"Uh," Claire added, "I guess I understand that. We'll have to see what we can arrange. Who takes her to the restaurant?"

"Some lady. I don know," Roscoe mumbled. And that was all they could get out of him.

Chapter 12: Hazel Reports In

Later that evening, Claire got a call from Hazel. She could hear ambient traffic sounds and the faint whistle from the wind that indicated Hazel was outside. "Where are you?" she asked.

"At a little park near my house sitting on a bench. I told my mother I felt like going for a walk and I'm using your new phone." Claire had given Hazel the promised burner phone with the ringer turned off so she couldn't receive incoming calls that would alert anyone around to the phone's presence. Hazel kept it buried deep in her purse. She was using it now for the first time and had carefully followed the instructions Claire had written out for her.

"What's happening?"

"There was another suspicious death today. I saw Inspector McCoy at the hospital and everybody was talking about it in the coffee room."

Claire gritted her teeth, annoyed that she hadn't been there when it had happened this time. But she knew why McCoy had been on the scene. Deaths at the hospital would have been flagged and he would have been called immediately, either by the staff as he'd instructed or by any responding officer.

"Do you know who died?"

"It was a man this time and one of the practical nurses who was in the coffee room said he was dementing and was very demanding all the time. Not a nice man, apparently."

"What was he so demanding about?" Claire asked, and held her breath.

"Oh, the nurse said he was always demanding to be taken to the bathroom, even though he was apparently incontinent."

"Can you find out how he died?" Claire asked.

"I could maybe ask that nurse. She seems really nice and she's the chatty type. She's the one who found him this time. She's a friend of Rita, the girl I ride to work with some days. Maybe I could ask Rita to ask her."

"No!" Claire said, somewhat more explosively than she'd intended. "You have to be really careful. Don't let on to *anyone* that you have more than an idle, gossipy interest. It's not *safe*."

"Okay, okay," Hazel responded impatiently. "I'm there again tomorrow and I'll try to hang around the coffee room more and see what else I can pick up. Maybe somebody will hear something."

"Yes, that's a good idea. But please don't forget and start talking and asking questions. Believe me, I know what can happen because it's happened to both Tia and me."

"I promise," Hazel said soberly, finally seeming to register the seriousness of the situation.

"Meanwhile, Tia or I will try to talk to Sergeant Crombie. He might tell us what happened." Claire hung up then. She was just finishing her work shift and she left directly for the hospital to visit Marisa. But when she arrived, everything was calm as if nothing had happened and Marisa was sleeping. She took the few soiled clothes she found in the hamper and headed for Tia's house. She thought there should still be a slight window of time before Jimmy arrived home and gave her the evil eye.

Of course, Tia was upset about the most recent murder, but she was happy to hear that Marisa was okay. "We have to do something more than we're doing, Claire, or we're never going to find this murderer, and I very much doubt that McCoy will either."

Claire nodded her head grimly. "We can't leave it all on the shoulders of a 19-year-old girl, eager as she is. But *what*?"

"We-e-ll," Tia said slowly. "You're not going to believe this, but I was perusing the want ads in the paper today. Marion is doing so much better that I figure I can leave her for periods of time if I get reliable help. Anyway, guess what ad I saw today?"

Claire responded, "Don't tell me they need a part-time housekeeper at the hospital?"

"Not a housekeeper. A head of housekeeping to work 20 hours a week, responsible for training and for maintaining standards."

"Wow! That would be *perfect* for you." And, after a beat, Claire added, "And I can just imagine what *Jimmy* will say."

Tia regarded her stonily. "Marion is okay now. I can stop worrying about her. And my next priority is my mother. He's going to *have* to understand that."

"Well, good luck with that," Claire said. Just then she heard Jimmy's van in the driveway and she got up hurriedly to leave.

As Claire had predicted, the conversation that evening at Tia's home was anything but tranquil. However, in the back of his mind, Jimmy had been seriously worried about Tia's mood and he was happy to see her being her old alert and energetic self again. And he too was concerned about Marisa. He was fond of Marisa but, more than that, he knew how important she was to Mario. So he gave up on this battle a little more readily than he had the previous ones, albeit with the same provisos—to be careful, to not trust anyone, to always keep her guard up, and not to end up in a room alone with her back to the door, as she'd already done twice previously.

The next morning, Tia phoned the Human Resources contact person listed in the hospital ad, but she had no doubt that she would get the job. Her references were excellent and her housekeeping skills had already been written up in a couple of newspaper articles. She met with Kay Shriver that very afternoon and in the evening, over supper, she reported to Jimmy and Mario that she had the position and would be beginning as soon as she had worked out appropriate care for Marion. In fact, their neighbor, Amanda, was coming over the next morning to spend the day and see if caring for the baby was something she could do.

"But she's had absolutely no childcare experience. She gave away her own son right after he was born. What good is she going to be?" Jimmy asked.

"It's karma," Tia replied softly. "Amanda has deep regrets about that to this day—and she definitely feels that she missed out on something very precious. I think caring for Marion can help her to heal that wound and she's anxious to help me so I can help find the killer and keep Marisa safe."

"You're right, Mom. I know Miss Roche. She's very sensible and level-headed. And she's also cautious. She's not going to let anything bad happen to Marion. And I'll come home right after school and stay close to Marion until you get home. I think it will be good for you to get out of this house. You haven't been yourself for a long time now," Mario interjected.

Tia smiled at him and ruffled his hair. Jimmy just rolled his eyes, but they were both thinking the same thoughts about their caring and precocious son. Marion began fussing then and Tia nursed her.

"How are you going to keep up the nursing if you're working 20 hours a week?" Jimmy asked. "Babies really need breast milk from everything I've heard."

"A lady in our mother's group is going to sell me her dual nursing pump. She says it's far superior to any other pump on the market and in 15 minutes, I'll be able to collect as much milk as I could do in an hour with my pump. And I'll only be away from her about five hours a day. It's not ideal but I think all things considered, this solution will be best for everyone including Marion. I'm looking forward to the job. Hazel has told me some stories about cleaning there and I know they need me."

Jimmy shrugged his shoulders in a gesture of defeat but secretly he was happy to see his old Tia back in the game. Mario then added in his two cents worth. "I think you should start practicing right now, Mom. Marion's going to be going to sleep soon and I can stay here with her. You take your cell phone and I promise to call you right away if something goes wrong. You and Jim-Dad go out to a movie or a lounge or something. I saw a sign in that Pub on the corner that they're having a well-known band there tonight. That could be fun and you guys need to start getting out more."

Jimmy grinned at him and said, "I think you're right, son. And there's something else I've been meaning to talk to you about. We've been together a couple of years now. Do you think I've passed the test and you could start just calling me 'Dad'?"

Mario's look was hard to read. He was sitting next to Jimmy at the table and Mario just reached over and put his arm around him. "Sure, Dad," he said in a muffled voice as he nestled into Jimmy's shoulder. Jimmy spontaneously kissed him on the cheek and hugged him hard. "Okay, now," he said. "We got to act like men. Remember that." Tia looked at them both with tears in her eyes as she automatically patted Marion's back, stretched over her shoulder. Just then Marion let out a big burp and they all laughed.

"I'll change Marion and get her ready for bed. And then we'll be off, Mario. I'll skip her bath tonight."

"I'm going to read to her until she goes to sleep," Mario said soberly. "You guys have fun."

And Jimmy and Tia did have fun. They enjoyed the music, had a couple of drinks and then called it a night. They felt closer to each other than they had for quite a while and their nighttime activities reflected that.

Chapter 13: Tia Gets to Work

The next day was a busy one for Tia and Amanda. It was focused partly around teaching Amanda the ins and outs of Marion's schedule, and partly around Tia satisfying herself that Amanda could and should be taking over for her. But, by the end of the day, Tia was at peace with the idea. She called Kay Shriver, the Human Resources officer she'd been dealing with, to tell her that she was prepared to begin work the next day and it was agreed that that would work and that she could flex her four hours each day as needed if there were any problems with the baby or the care arrangements.

The next morning, Tia was happy to see that she could still fit into her work wardrobe, clothes she hadn't worn since before her pregnancy. After she arrived at the hospital, her first stop was to check in with Kay in order to sign some papers. She'd already had a tour of the facility during her previous visit and had been informed about the routine and where supplies were kept. Tia asked Kay to set up a brief meeting at eleven with the three housekeeping staff on duty that day. Two others were off, one being Hazel, and she would catch up with them another time.

As she walked slowly through the hospital armed with her new set of keys that allowed her access to the supply closets and to the locked unit on the third floor reserved for advanced Alzheimer's patients, Tia felt her shoulders lifting and her lungs expanding. It was good to be out of the house and back to work. She realized suddenly that simple housekeeping no longer satisfied her the way it once had.

She needed a challenge—and more material for the book she was writing.

Her first task was to check the cleaning supplies. Their type and condition would definitely have an impact on how clean things could be kept. She tried out various vacuum cleaners and checked them over for condition. She also surveyed the collection of mops she found and was not too happy with them. The type of soap being used was not her favorite either, because of its high suds content and strong odor, and there was no evidence of a separate set of bathroom cleaning supplies.

Tia had only arrived at 9:30 that morning, after making sure that Marion was well settled in with Amanda, and eleven o'clock was approaching fast. She braced herself for the upcoming meeting. She'd learned the hard way from her previous experiences that the head-on approach was not wise. Besides, Kay had mentioned that she'd informed the staff about Tia's background, so this time she had no need to prove herself. Her goal was to convince them to like and trust her so they would go along more readily with her suggestions. Even so, she knew there would probably be at least one holdout.

Tia began by introducing herself and telling the women a little about her background, her passion for cleaning and her book project that she had tentatively entitled, "Cleaning it Right." Then she asked them to introduce themselves and tell her something about their own background and how and why they'd chosen to take the job at the hospital.

Anna Weisman spoke first. She had a strong accent and explained that she was an immigrant from the former republic of Czechoslovakia and this was the only job she could get in Edmonton despite the fact that she had an undergraduate degree from the University of Prague in Chemistry. "Fortunately, my mother was a cleaning fanatic and I learned at a young age how to clean." Anna then described some of her favorite cleaning techniques, not all of which Tia agreed with. However, she knew this time the value of holding her tongue and instead sincerely complemented Anna on her enthusiasm and desire to do a good job

The next person who spoke was Rita Fisher. She was the friend who'd offered to drive Hazel to work and Tia regarded her carefully. Rita confessed that she'd had trouble learning in school and had dropped out in Grade 11. She was basically here because it was the only job she could get. However, she was resolved to make the best of it and do a decent job—although she made it clear that she was no cleaning fanatic. She took her breaks religiously and cut corners when necessary in order to get her assigned work done in the time allotted.

Unlike Anna, who, despite her modest cleaning garb, managed to look neat and clean and professional, Rita's presentation was quite different. First of all, she was chewing gum that she occasionally popped. Secondly, her blond hair was pulled back carelessly in a rough ponytail and the roots were very obviously showing. And thirdly, she was wearing jeans that were a little too tight and a top that was on the skimpy side. Long earrings dangled from her ears. Tia silently debated with herself whether or not she should introduce a dress code but decided she had other priorities—for the time being at least.

The last person to speak was an older, stocky, grey-haired lady with the remnants of an Irish accent. Her name was Myrtle O'Hare, and Tia knew right away that she was going to be the holdout. Myrtle quickly introduced herself and then declared in strident tones, "I've been here at this hospital for twenty years now so I'm pretty sure I know how to clean—but if I'm going to get my work done today I don't have more time for talk."

The other two cleaners looked at each other, each well aware that Myrtle always had time for talk in the coffee room—and quite a lot of time at that. Tia just replied,

"Your sense of duty is admirable, Myrtle, but this is important. If you don't get all your work done today, we will understand, but there are a few things I want to discuss while I have you all here."

Tia looked at the others, then and commented, "I've been checking out the cleaning supplies and equipment and before I make any comment I'd like to hear from you. Anna, do you see any room for improvement there?"

Before Anna could respond, Myrtle jumped in, making it clear by her tone that as the senior cleaner she should be the first one to speak. "The vacs are a pile of junk. Some of them hardly work at all."

"Thank you for pointing that out, Myrtle. I'll be checking them all over to see if some need replacing or just reconditioning. How often do you change the bags?"

"No sense wasting. I tell the other girls to fill 'em right up."

Tia realized two things at that point. In the unstructured system that had been operating at the hospital, Myrtle, by the combined weight of her body, age and personality, had set herself up as the informal head of housekeeping. Thus, no matter what she did or said, Tia would be seen as an interloper and a threat. And, of course, from what Myrtle had said, she already had a pretty good idea of what was wrong with the vacuum cleaners.

But how can I put it? she asked herself. Instead of responding directly to what Myrtle had said, Tia turned back to Anna. "Anna, what annoys you the most about the current equipment and supplies?"

"Well, it's true that the vacuums don't work as well as they could, but it's the mops that irritate me the most. You just can't get into the corners with them or do the baseboards properly and if you try you just stain up the walls."

"Yes, I agree with you, Anna. In the brief time I had to check out the equipment this morning, I had the same opinion about the mops. I'll be looking into some possible replacements."

"Don't you be gettin' any of them skinny little mops. It'll take three times as long to do the job," Myrtle demanded in bellicose tones.

"I'll take your concern into consideration, Myrtle," Tia replied mildly.

Rita spoke up then, recognizing that it was her turn. "I don't really have any complaints about the equipment. I just make do with what I have. Oh," she added, after a pause, "it would be nice to bring in those Swiffer dusters. I get kind of sick of dragging that same rag over everything and having to trot outside to shake it every once in awhile."

Tia felt her insides trembling when she heard this but struggled to maintain a neutral face. "I will be definitely look into that," she replied. "Thanks for pointing it out, Rita."

Myrtle could not resist jumping in again. "There's nothing wrong with a good, old-fashioned duster. All this new fangled stuff is just an expensive waste."

I can see I'll have my hands full with her, Tia thought to herself. But aloud she just said, "I have been here too short a time to have anything meaningful to add to this conversation, but I want to thank you all for sharing your concerns. I suggest that we meet again next Monday and meanwhile I'll talk to the two cleaners who are away today and get their input.

"I'll be coming around to shadow each of you over the next couple of days just to get a feel for what's happening and see what I can come up with that will make things easier for everybody and still get the job done we all want."

They parted then and Tia went off to have a word with Kay. Myrtle was very convincing in her authoritarian way and Tia wanted to gauge how much support she would have from Human Resources if it became necessary to go head to head with her on certain issues. But she need not have worried about Kay's support.

"Myrtle's quite the know-it-all but she's not one of our better cleaners. In fact, some days she spends more time in the coffee room than on the wards. You do what you have to do to shape this place up. That's what we hired you for. And we *had* to do that because we have actually had complaints from the health inspector. Don't worry about Myrtle. Everybody knows how she operates. If she can't take the heat and decides to quit it will be no great loss. And if she refuses to listen to you, I'll see that she's disciplined and that it's written up in her file. I think the reason she came on so strong today is because she's afraid and wanted to intimidate you so you wouldn't try to cross her."

After leaving Kay, Tia felt much better and spent the rest of her shift on her own trying out the various pieces of equipment. Kay had given her the stack of catalogues advertising cleaning supplies that had been sent to the hospital at various times. It didn't bode well that catalogues several years old were included, most still in their original plastic covers.

Tia wrote down the names of the different cleaning companies from the catalogues, but then left them behind in the tiny office she'd been assigned. That evening, she spent a couple of hours of her own time checking out their websites and familiarizing herself with the new materials that had become available in the two years since she'd been actively involved in the cleaning business.

At nine that evening, Claire called. "I talked to Hazel today to let her know what was happening with you being at the hospital. I warned her not to let on that she knows you when you see her tomorrow. I have to tell you, Tia, that she sounded a little miffed, like you were replacing her as the resident snoop."

"Thanks for the heads up, Claire. I'll sort it out with her tomorrow. I have the perfect excuse to talk to her privately in my office since I told the other cleaners I'd be meeting with the two who were missing today. I'll keep them each in my office the same length of time but I'll arrange with Hazel to meet with her privately outside of work and discuss a plan of action, for the cleaning issues, maybe divide up the territory. Fortunately, I'll now have control of scheduling cleaning responsibilities."

"Sounds good," Claire replied. "And *you* sound good. I can just tell by your voice that it's good for you to be back at work. Did Marion do alright with Amanda today?"

"Disgustingly well." Tia laughed. "I don't think Marion even missed me. And Amanda seemed really chipper when I came home, like she'd been enjoying herself. I just hope it lasts and the novelty doesn't wear off."

"Amanda's pretty steady. If she promised to do it, I'm sure she'll carry through. And anyway, you aren't planning to do this forever—just till you find the killer, right?"

"I don't know," Tia said. "I think I've had enough of being a home body."

"What about Marion and the nursing? From what I know, if you don't keep at that very consistently you can lose your milk supply pretty fast."

"I plan to pump every night and I'll carry on as long as I can. But one way or another, I'm going to keep it up until Marion is at least six months old, and if I have to revert to formula after that it won't be the end of the world. She'll have had a good start—and the way I'm feeling right now, I think it's better for the whole family for me to be happy, than just to be a milk machine."

"I agree, Tia," Claire responded, "and it's so great to hear you sounding like your old self. I've missed you."

"Yeah, it's definitely nice to be back. Well, I better get to sleep now so I can be fresh for tomorrow. I'm going to have to be on my toes to deal with Myrtle."

"Who's Myrtle?"

"Another time, Claire. Maybe we can get together for coffee on the weekend and I'll tell you all about her."

They signed off then and Tia made the necessary preparations for the next day. She went to sleep early with a smile on her face. Jimmy looked at her fondly when he came to bed, realizing himself that this was what she'd been missing. He would have dearly loved some together time but decided it was best just to let her sleep.

Chapter 14: Claire Gets Serious

Claire's cell phone rang the next day just as she and Roscoe were organizing themselves to go to the Arts Centre and visit Sarah Hughes, the director, who'd been so instrumental in helping Roscoe overcome the trauma of witnessing his friend being murdered.

It was Sergeant Crombie. "Claire, I promised I'd call you when we got the results of the autopsy back on Mr. Hall. He was definitely murdered. This time it was a poison placed in the cup of hot chocolate he had that evening in bed. Fortunately, we had the presence of mind to grab it when we were called to the scene."

"What kind of poison?" Claire asked.

"Antifreeze. It had been mixed with cocoa and milk to make hot chocolate because antifreeze is quite sweet by itself. It only takes about 1/3 of a cup of antifreeze to kill someone. When we checked through the hospital garbage bin, we found the discarded thermos. It was likely mixed at the murderer's home and carried in."

"Why do you think this particular man was targeted?"

"We don't know. The only thing we've found out that he had in common with the other two victims is that he tended to complain a lot."

"I see," Claire said, but didn't express her thoughts further.

After the phone call, Claire decided that she better change her plans and visit Marisa. She dropped Roscoe off at the restaurant so he could take over at the cash register during the mid-morning lull and told him she'd get someone else to cover his afternoon shift there so the two of them could visit the art gallery then.

Roscoe was happy with that plan and as soon as Claire left him, he ordered a piece of his favorite coconut cream pie. Since Roscoe was the owner of the restaurant, nobody but Claire felt they could ask him if he thought that a mid-morning piece of pie while he was technically on duty was a good idea.

Claire was surprised to find Marisa sitting in the wheelchair/lounge combination chair that the hospital kept for its patients who were non-ambulatory but able to be out of bed. This was the first time Claire had seen Marisa in it and Claire could see by the look on her face that she was unusually alert this morning. But a further surprise awaited her. "Ullo, Claih," Marisa said, her speech slurred from the residual effects of her recent stroke.

This was the first time Marisa had greeted Claire since her stroke. Claire rushed over and threw her arms around her declaring with gusto, "Welcome back, Marisa."

Marisa reflexively drew back, demonstrating the memory of her more formal upbringing and Claire immediately apologized. But Marisa just smiled at her, albeit a bit crookedly. Claire talked then with Marisa occasionally adding in one-word rejoinders but soon she was tired out by the effort and a nurse came to transfer her back into bed with the assistance of a hospital orderly. Marisa was trying to say something to them that sounded like 'bathroom,' but they studiously ignored her, telling her that she needed to sleep. Claire left with a niggling fear in her mind.

That day when she got home from work, Claire informed Dan that she needed to talk to him and they should sit down together with a glass of wine before dinner since Mia was there looking after Jessie.

"Okay," he said grudgingly. "But no wine for me. I still have work to do."

"Okay," Claire said, tight lipped. "I'll meet you in ten minutes in your study." She could never decide if she admired or hated Dan's temperate habits and high level of self-control. It seemed to her that just dealing with Jessie's various challenges provided enough moral discipline in their lives without taking the rest of the joy out of it. But now was not the time to have that discussion.

Claire went into the family room to talk to Jessie who was listening to an Andrea Boccelli aria on her sound system. Jessie clearly enjoyed music, especially classical music and particularly the sounds of male tenors. Dan had provided her with every cd of Boccelli he could find and, as Claire listened to the singer's moaning, 'high opera' voice, she gritted her teeth. Not her favorite. That was for sure. But Jessie enjoyed him and smiled at Claire in her sweet way.

After telling Jessie about her day and checking the communication book from school, Claire headed to the study with her glass of wine and a small handful of nuts. She didn't bring any for Dan who'd only have said it would spoil his supper, and she didn't bring along the crackers and cheese she would have preferred, not to mention the wine bottle. Such actions would only have caused him to raise his eyebrows at her over her "unnecessary self-indulgence" as he liked to put it.

"Well, what did you want to talk about?" Dan inquired. "How was your day?" he asked perfunctorily.

"There was a third murder at the hospital last week."

"Last week? Why didn't you mention it before?"

"The autopsy results just came back this morning. They were really backed up over at the morgue apparently."

"I'm sorry to hear that," Dan said slowly. "Is Marisa okay?"

"Yes, in fact she seems to be improving—but that may be the problem."

"What do you mean?"

"Today she was talking a bit for the first time and sitting in a chair. When the nurse and orderly lifted her back into bed, I heard her say, 'bathroom' but they just ignored her."

"Well, she's probably too weak to sit on a toilet yet, anyway."

"Yes, but I don't think she will be for long. And I *know* her. She's a very fastidious lady. She's not going to tolerate being fobbed off when she needs bathroom access."

"So? Why is that a problem?"

"Because the three people who have been killed to date all regularly complained about needing to use the bathroom and they wouldn't give in and just use their diaper until they absolutely had to."

"But that's a *good* thing, *surely*!"

"You'd think so, but not in that place."

"Because?"

"Because it's a big bother and very labor intensive for staff to place someone who is physically helpless on a commode. First of all, Occupational Health and Safety Rules require that two staff members be present at all times when a floor lift's in use. Then, after the patient is hoisted up in the lift sling, they're usually transported to their bed and lowered onto it so it can function as a change table. Then staff have to lift the person up again once they're undressed and transfer them to a commode in a space not large enough to move the lift around easily. And by the time they get around to that, the person is usually wet or soiled or sometimes feel like they no longer need to go."

"So what happens then?"

"They redress the person and reverse the process. But going through all that takes twenty minutes or longer so you can imagine why they're anxious to get people into diapers. That way it's a far simpler process. They just hoist them up with the lift, wheel them into their bedroom, dump them down on the bed, change them, hoist them up and return them to their chairs.

"Well, what else can they do?"

"Tell me, Dan. How would you feel if that was happening to Jessie?"

"Not good. But it isn't happening and it's not likely to happen any time soon since she's barely into her teens and far from being a senior citizen who's destined for an extended care hospital."

"Well, it's happening to Marisa."

"I'm sorry about that but I don't see what we can do."

"The loss of dignity is bad enough but we're also talking about loss of life here. There have been three murders."

"I don't see the connection?"

"Everyone killed so far has been a complainer. Specifically, they've complained endlessly about needing to go to the bathroom and refused to just sink back into incontinence."

"Are you saying that somebody is killing them just to save a few extra minutes."

"That seems the most likely possibility right now."

"Well, if that's so, it certainly narrows the suspect pool. It would have to be one of the direct care providers. The nurses and doctors don't do that kind of work."

"Probably—but that's not my main concern right now." Dan raised his eyebrows but Claire went on, "My concern is Marisa. She's becoming more aware every day—and she's not going to tolerate being treated as though she were incontinent for long."

"But I recall Marisa as being a very refined, polite kind of woman. She doesn't seem like the victims you've been describing."

"That's not true. Mrs. Burbidge was a nice person. She was just insistent and Marisa is likely to be that way, too."

"You've done what you can to protect her, Claire. You have visitors going in for hours every day."

"But she's still alone at night and these murders have all taken place between late evening and early morning."

"Okay. It seems to me that narrows the suspect pool even further. I can't believe I'm saying this but maybe you better put your energies into identifying the killer. Then the problem will be solved."

"Sure. Then they won't destroy her body. They'll only destroy her soul," Claire said, somewhat dramatically.

"Well, what do you see as the answer then?" Dan asked, and immediately bit his tongue. Somehow he knew that he'd just walked into the trap Claire had been so carefully laying for him.

"Marisa doesn't belong there at all. As soon as she is a bit better, she should be at home."

"Back in Wetaskiwin?"

"No. Obviously, that's not an answer since her stroke. She needs to be here, close to all of us. And she'll need access to some special facilities."

"Where exactly?" Dan asked, although he wasn't sure he wanted to hear the answer.

"We-e-ll. I've been thinking," Claire began slowly. Dan braced himself. Claire went on. "She and Alberto *could* stay with us for a bit while Jimmy and Tia have an extra room and bath built onto the back of their house. Their back yard is huge and there's plenty of room for an extension. She could share Jessie's raised bath and ceiling lift and change table."

Claire stopped then because Dan was shaking his head vigorously.

"Why not?" she asked, somewhat belligerently. "Don't you ever feel like we should do something for somebody *else*?"

"You do plenty for other people. You always *have*!"

"What about you? I can't do any more for Marisa without your help."

"I don't want anybody else living in our house. Don't we have little enough privacy as it is with Jessie's assistants in and out all the time?"

"Okay, have you got a better idea?" But Dan just looked at her blankly.

"Look, Dan," Claire said, "I understand your point and I feel the same way basically. If Marisa is anywhere but the hospital, she should be with her daughter."

"How could *that* work?" Dan asked. "They don't have the room and they don't have the facilities."

"Well, that's where we *could* help." It was clear from his face that Dan regarded the 'we' with suspicion but Claire went on anyway. "You're an architect. And you know what we've had to do in order to meet Jessie's needs. It wouldn't take you much time and effort to draft out a plan for an extension on Tia's house. And we could lend them our floor lift for the time being. We don't use it much since we got the ceiling lift. We can just do a two-person lift with the hammock sling when we need to. Jessie is light enough."

"You *know* how hard it is to get somebody into bed with a floor lift because of their big wheels."

"Ah, but you don't know Tia's guest room bed. It's an old fashioned double bed on wheels with a slat spring so there's plenty of room underneath for the lift wheels. All Tia will need to do is get a good, firm mattress and probably a nice, cushy mattress topper and a waterproof mattress cover just in case."

"That would certainly solve one big problem. You can't be doing with Marisa like we've had to do with Jessie sometimes when travelling—maneuver her onto the corner of the bed with our portable floor lift and then wiggle her into position. Marisa would be too stiff and fragile for that kind of treatment. You could end up breaking her bones."

Claire relaxed a bit. It sounded like Dan was beginning to buy in. "Of course, then there's the toileting issue," she added cautiously.

"Uh huh," Dan replied grimly, thinking of the labor-intensive nature of their daily life with Jessie. "How do you expect Tia to cope with all those lifts and transfers and look after baby Marion at the same time?"

"I've been worrying about that," Claire replied, "and I think there's only one solution."

"What?" Dan said, bracing himself.

"We're just going to have to perfect the lift and commode system in Jessie's wheelchair and develop one for Marisa like it."

"With what money?"

"Marisa and Alberto have some money. Tia *told* me so."

"100,000.00 dollars? Because that's what it will take."

"I think so. They have money put aside for their retirement."

"And how do you know they're going to be willing to throw it all into a wheelchair?"

"It's not going to be 'they.' Marisa is not able to make decisions right now. It will be up to her husband. Alberto's so desperate to get Marisa back home, I think he'd do anything within his power to make that happen."

"Well, Tia might have something to say about it and I think he'd listen to her."

"Tia is overwhelmed with guilt and grief over her mother. Having Marisa with her, no matter how hard, would be less of a burden than the one she's currently carrying."

Dan looked thoughtful. "It's not just money we're talking about here. A chair with a built-in lift for Marisa is going to look a lot different than the one we developed for Jessie. She's old and stiff and she can't just be juggled around in a lift chair to make it work the way we do with Jessie."

"I *know* all that," Claire said impatiently. "But there *has* to be a way."

Chapter 15: Hazel and Tia Work out a Plan

On Tuesday morning, Tia met with Clara Borge, one of the missing housekeepers at the first meeting. Clara was a thin, washed out-looking woman. Tia judged her to be only in her early 40's but she already had deep wrinkles in her forehead. Once she came to know Clara a little better, Tia understood why. She was always worrying about her delinquent son or her alcoholic husband or her promiscuous, 16-year-old daughter. At work, Clara did her job grimly and dutifully but with no particular passion or imagination. When asked what she would like to see changed, all Clara could suggest was to start using liquid soap because the bar soap in the patient washrooms made the counters and sinks more difficult to clean. At the end of the meeting, Tia asked, "What do you think about the murders that have been happening in the hospital, and Clara's response surprised and chilled her.

"What did they have to live for, anyway? Maybe whoever is doing this is actually doing them a favor. *I* wouldn't want to live like that."

Tia's meeting with Hazel at ten was a much more positive one despite a little tension at the beginning. It was clear that Hazel was feeling miffed because she saw Tia as supplanting her role.

"Look, Hazel," Tia said, "I can see you're wondering why we both need to be working on the murders at this end. But there's a good reason. You need to remain deep under cover as the resident mole. Everyone knows my mother is here and probably just assume I'll be anxious about her safety—and I am. That means I can ask certain questions that you can't without expressing a suspicious amount of interest, and people might be more willing to talk to you than me. So let's figure out how to divide the work so we can get the job done. And the first thing we need to figure out is where, when and how we can talk safely so we can keep in close communication."

Hazel was somewhat mollified after this explanation and for the next ten minutes they discussed strategy.

"We can't make this meeting much longer or it'll look suspicious," Tia said then. "Any quick thoughts on ways to improve our cleaning operation?"

"I have a number of ideas," Hazel replied. "But I wrote them out for you to save time. I suggest we discuss them later in private so as not to stay in your office here too long. I figured we would be spending our time on this other issue."

Tia looked at her appreciatively and commented, "I think we're going to work very well together." She glanced quickly at the paper, raised her eyebrows once and smiled a moment later. Then she got up and opened the door. "Thanks for coming in, Hazel, and sharing your ideas for improvement. I will certainly be considering them."

After Hazel left, Tia sat at her desk and reviewed her notes on the comments she'd received from the cleaners along with Hazel's written suggestions. She could see right away that Hazel had the most thoughtful, systems-oriented view. She obviously had a genuine interest in the art of cleaning.

Once she'd reviewed all her notes, Tia set out to do her own critical analysis of the situation, establish her priorities, prepare an inventory of equipment and supplies and begin formulating an order list. She knew what Claire would be saying if she were watching—that this was not the primary reason Tia was here. But Tia knew from past experience that her first task was to establish her credibility and her value to the organization. If she didn't do that, she would never have a strong enough foothold with the other hospital personnel to truly be a part of things. Also, establishing a reputation for being thorough gave her a plausible reason to snoop into every corner—something Hazel couldn't do since each cleaner had her assigned tasks.

Tia's first stop was the hospital kitchen. Technically speaking, supervision of overall kitchen sanitation was not part of her mandate. There were government inspectors for that. But her staff was responsible for floor, wall and window cleaning. Tia looked around and talked to the one kitchen staff present at the time. When she left to carry a special meal to one of the patients, Tia took the opportunity to quickly check through the cupboards to get a feel for the way things were kept, just on the off chance she might run across any antifreeze or spare hypodermic needles or injectable drugs.

The kitchen staff person, whose name was Liz, returned before she could complete her search, however. Tia asked her if the kitchen was open 24 hours and if there were always kitchen personnel working there. She explained that she needed to identify the best times for her staff to do the necessary wall cleaning, making several *tsking* noises over a few spots she found on the walls as she spoke.

"The kitchen is closed from eleven at night until five in the morning," Liz replied. "No staff work during those hours."

"Is it locked then?" Liz nodded her head. "How would my staff gain access?"

"My understanding is that the cleaning department has a kitchen key. You were probably given it when you started."

Tia nodded her head slowly. "I haven't had time yet to identify all the keys. So you're saying that you think it would be alright if we cleaned the walls at night?"

"Well, I've been here five years and I've never seen *anyone* from the cleaning staff cleaning the walls.

Occasionally, when things get too bad one of us gives the worst spots a quick swipe."

"Well, we'll see about that," Tia said, nodding her head soberly. She left then, filing the information away for future reference. If she ever felt that the kitchen held possible clues, she'd bring in Hazel one evening and in two hours they could get those walls clean and the place thoroughly searched. Tia felt quite sure of that.

By the end of that day, Tia had a pretty good idea of what was being done well in terms of cleaning at the hospital and what was not. By reviewing the cleaning roster for the past two months, she was also able to gain a strong sense of who was cleaning properly and who was not, since they all had their set areas of responsibility.

Over the next week, Tia had the vacuum cleaner technician out to check over the machines. It was soon apparent that they'd all been misused to a greater or lesser extent. He was able to overhaul a few, but the rest had to be replaced. Fortunately, the local company was able to provide the replacements within a couple of days.

When Myrtle, Anna, Rita, Hazel and Clara filed into the next meeting, they were surprised and pleased to see five new vacuum cleaners on display. The technician was also present to explain about proper care and maintenance. Tia noticed that Myrtle kept sniffing and rolling her eyes while he was speaking and Rita had a bored look on her face and chewed her gum vigorously. Only Anna and Hazel appeared to be paying close attention while Clara sat quietly with her chronic look of nervous preoccupation. But Tia had a surprise for them.

After the technician finished speaking and had answered a couple of questions from Hazel and Anna, Tia thanked him and he left. Then she turned the machines around, revealing that each machine had been labeled with one of the cleaner's names. "These are to be stored in your lockers when not in use," she told them. "You will be responsible for their maintenance and need to report any problems with them to me as soon as possible. You cannot clean properly without a good machine, but vacuums don't stay efficient for very long if they are abused. A copy of the maintenance suggestions will be posted in your workroom in case you need to refresh your memory," Tia said, looking steadily at Myrtle and Rita. "The reconditioned vacuum cleaners are being stored away for emergency use when a replacement is required or when we have a substitute staff member working."

Tia was the first to leave the room after the meeting, knowing that the cleaners might want a few minutes to discuss this policy change among themselves. Just before she'd completely closed the door, Tia heard Myrtle proclaiming in a loud voice, "And here I thought Nazi Germany was behind us!"

Tia had needed to access general hospital funds for the money to purchase the new vacuum cleaners, as her cleaning budget could not begin to cover the cost. She had argued strongly that there was no way to achieve the cleaning standards they were hoping for without them but had also explained her plans for maintaining them. Part of her argument had been to pull out a tally of the almost $2000.00 in repair costs for the existing vacuums over the past year, some of which were only two or three years old.

"We need to start fresh with new machines," Tia had explained to the hospital director and several department heads who'd convened to hear this special budget request. "But this time we need to hold the cleaners accountable for their proper upkeep. We may lose some of them in the process but the ones who really want to clean properly will stay." This brought knowing grins from the senior staff present. They had a pretty good sense of which cleaners did the job well and which did not.

Tia had succeeded in receiving general hospital funds for the machines, but for anything else she'd have to draw on her own meager cleaning budget. Therefore, she considered what to purchase very carefully. She did buy the skinny mops—a modest purchase under $100.00 in total—but asked the staff to use them for the floorboards, tight spots, corners and bathroom floors only and to keep using the big mops for the large areas. This particular cleaning revolution happened at yet another staff meeting and this time, Myrtle's odd *humph* was less frequent and less derisive than the ones emitted during the vacuum cleaner introductory event.

Chapter 16: No More Time!

By the time Tia had been at the hospital for a few weeks, things were running quite smoothly. However, she knew not one thing more about the murderer than she had when she first came. Meanwhile, Marisa had been improving steadily and was now able to sit up in a special hospital chair that reclined and could be moved around on its small castor wheels. But with her improvement came a new and worrisome problem.

Marisa was now aware enough to want assistance to attend to her bathroom needs in a proper manner, but the staff resisted, offering all kinds of excuses that she was still too weak, that she might get injured and so forth. By nature a polite and patient lady, Marisa had gone along with this at first but was slowly realizing her own growing strength and was becoming increasingly insistent on using a toilet or commode. Claire saw this too and had convinced Dan that they absolutely had to get the wheelchair/lift/commode unit settled so they could bring Marisa home to Tia's house.

Then the inevitable happened and there was another suspected murder. Again it was in Marisa's unit of the hospital although not in her room and again the victim was somebody who was quite vocal about bathroom needs. Tia was beside herself and when she saw Sergeant Crombie talking to the nurse who'd found the body, she interrupted almost rudely, demanding to know how the man had died and when would they know for sure if it was a murder or not.

Crombie and the nurse could both see the panic in Tia's eyes. He excused himself, saying he'd catch up to her later at the nursing station, and turned towards Tia. "The man who died appears to have been smothered by his pillow. He was quite frail and it's possible it was an accident or maybe even a heart attack. We'll have to wait for the coroner's report to know for sure. If petechial hemorrhaging is present that will be a positive indicator. We couldn't tell for sure because apparently his eyes are always quite red and bloodshot-looking. I'll let you know as soon as I hear," he assured Tia. Then he patted her on the shoulder and turned towards the nursing station. Tia walked off without a word. She was too upset to even thank him for taking the time to talk to her.

When she heard the news, Claire organized an emergency meeting at Tia's home for that evening at seven. Amanda was there to take care of Marion. Claire had invited Amanda's grandson, Matthew, as well because of his computer expertise. Roscoe was present with his father, Fuji, his brother Randy, and Randy's two sons, Thomas and Gerald, who were both studying mechanical engineering at the University of Alberta. And Dan was there as well, along with both of Jessie's modified wheelchairs. Alberto was present and so was Mario, now eleven. The agenda was clear. Somehow, some way they had to get Marisa out of that hospital very soon.

Claire and Dan began by explaining what they'd accomplished to date with Jessie's wheelchair with the built-in lift and built-in commode and why it had been so important to do it. Claire began with her favorite oration on how useless handicap washrooms were to people who couldn't do a standing or seat-to-seat transfer because of muscle weakness or paralysis, and the kinds of lifestyle restrictions and resulting indignities this led to. Tia cut her off impatiently after a minute or two. "We get it. We know there's no other way. Let's move on." Claire forgave Tia her impatience because she knew how desperately worried she was about her mother.

Dan spoke then, quickly and efficiently explaining the long process they'd been through to build and refine the two prototype chair systems, and demonstrating to the group how they worked. He also commented on the differences between Jessie's still relatively flexible and healthy body and Marisa's stiffened body and fragile bones. *(See Appendix for a complete description of the dignity chair)*

"This new chair makes the whole toileting process about as dignified as it can get under the circumstances," Claire said. "I'd just love to have one like it for Marisa," she added wistfully.

Dan looked at Alberto who was suddenly leaning forward, clearly trying to figure out how to make that happen. "Forget it, Alberto. For the engineer to make a chair like this that would supposedly work for Marisa would cost more than $100,000.00. And even then, we can't be sure it would work. We've never experimented in these chairs with anyone as stiff as she now is, and Claire tells me she also has some osteoporosis. No, the first chair we showed you is the only one that we know will be safe for her. And she can have it for as long as she needs it. Jessie's not using it anymore now that she has the new one."

"That chair will work around the house," Claire said, "and you could travel with it from one place to another. But disassembling and reassembling it for daily outings would quickly become a tedious chore and many 'handicap washrooms' in public places wouldn't have the space to accommodate it. However, Marisa should be able to sit in it comfortably if we make some minor adjustments."

"When could you have it ready for mamma to try?" Tia asked excitedly.

"Dan and I are going to take it up to the hospital tomorrow to get the measurements when Marisa is in it, check for pressure points and proper seat depth and foot rest height, things like that. We aren't seating specialists but we've been through the process enough times with Jessie that we pretty well know what to look for. We have a lot of left over wheelchair seating materials at home and several good seating cushions so we should be able to make it usable in a few days. It's Thursday now and I'm hoping to have it ready to go by next Tuesday at the latest so we can bring her home."

"What about a sling?"

"We have plenty of toilet slings, experiments that didn't work out for Jessie, but they may work better for Marisa because she's a little bigger than Jessie. We'll take a couple with us tomorrow and figure out the right length for the support straps."

"What about baths?" Alberto asked. "Marisa does like her bath."

"Until we get the extension built, we'll have to take Marisa across the street to use Mavis' raised bath. We'd like to install a jet tub for Marisa, too, Alberto, and this will give her a chance to try it out to see if she likes it."

"And the extension? How long will that take to build?"

"Once we can all agree on the plans, I can draw them up in a couple of days," Dan said. "And Jimmy and I were discussing today how much of the work we could do ourselves and what we'd have to hire trades people to do."

"We are helping out," Fuji said. "I'm not much use in the restaurant but I can sure do this."

"We're all going to help," chimed in Randy and his two sons."

"Me, too," said Roscoe. "I hep."

"I don't think so, Roscoe," Claire said. "You're the busiest one of all of us between your maître d' and cashier work at the restaurant and your volunteer work at the hospital. Let the rest of them do *this*."

"You can keep us in cookies and coffee, Roscoe. That will help a lot to keep us going," Gerald suggested.

Roscoe looked at Gerald soberly. "Claih and I make cookies and bwing them. Wight, Claih?"

"Yes—and we will borrow that big thermos from the restaurant to bring the coffee over."

"And when you're all done, as rewawd, I bwing coconut cweam pie from restauwant," Roscoe added, with a big grin.

"Sounds *good*," Roscoe's nephews responded together.

"But what do we do in the meantime?" Tia wanted to know. "What about when I'm at work?"

"Don't worry. I've got that covered," Claire assured her. Marisa is going to spend the days with us across the street. Mavis is going to share her facilities so Marisa can start every day with a nice, soothing jet bath to get her stiff muscles warmed up. Then she can keep Roscoe and me company while I do bookwork and he does some homework."

"And then I take Marisa for walk," Roscoe added. "*I* know how."

Tia looked at him doubtfully but then Jimmy chimed in. "I'm sure you will do at *least* as good a job as Gus did with Jessie." Everybody laughed but the humor was rather dark, considering that they all knew that Aunt Gus had once sent Jessie careening down a hill in her wheelchair, right into the arms of a killer!

Chapter 17: The Immediate Situation

Tia wanted to move away from the talk of house renovation and return to the pressing issue of getting Marisa out of the hospital as soon as possible and providing appropriate care for her. "If my parents are going to move in with us, then we have to put their house up for sale and that means that I have to go out there with the baby and help dad clear it out. I'm going to have to take at least a week off work to do that. And what will we do with la mamma then? And how are we going to manage here anyway with all those renovations going on? Mom is still very weak and fragile. And she has already had one stroke. We can't risk stressing her."

Claire sat there silently. For once she had no answer. She could bring Marisa over during the day. She could legitimately make it a volunteer job for Mavis, sharing her facilities and her staff for a few hours. But she couldn't exactly move Marisa in there. *Pushing the envelope is one thing,* Claire said to herself, *but this would be like crushing it up and throwing it out the window. It could put our whole program in jeopardy.*

Eleven-year old Mario had been listening quietly to this exchange and now he spoke up. "Excuse me, but I have something to say, please."

"Yes, Mario?" Tia asked, patiently but with a note of irritation in her voice.

"As you know, I have stayed with nonno and nonna many times out in Wetaskiwin and I know how they live, mamma. It is not like us. They like to get up late. They like to have the radio on in the morning to listen to the farm report—and it is quite loud. I think they both don't hear as well as they used to. And they like lifebuoy soap which has a very strong smell—and *you* don't like smelly soap."

"And your point is?" Tia interrupted. She was feeling very tense with all her worries over Marisa and didn't have the patience to listen any longer to Mario.

"Well, that's just it, you see. I don't think they'll be happy living with us."

"Well what would you suggest?" Jimmy asked wearily. "They can't live alone anymore without support."

"I think they need to live near us but not with us. If they lived nearby this whole community that you have all built up could be their support."

"Where?" Tia asked with growing impatience. "Look, Mario, there's no time left for dreaming. We have to act. We have to get la nonna out of that hospital."

Mario looked at them all. "I have a solution. I have been visiting with Mr. Hendricks next door. As you know, he has been living alone since his wife died three years ago. He never wanted to leave his house, but his son, who lives with his family in Kelowna, B. C., has been begging him to move out there. I explained to him that if he would sell his house to us then he could come and visit it whenever he wanted and I said we could even keep some of his favorite furniture since he couldn't take it with him and that way he could…"

"You *what?*" Tia demanded. All the frustration and rage she'd been struggling with inside herself threatened to bubble over. She even went so far as to raise her hand as if to strike Mario, and Jimmy quickly stepped in to intervene.

Claire jumped up then and stood beside Mario with her arm firmly around him. Alberto was also on his feet by this time and hovering over Mario protectively. "*Wait, Tia!* Calm down and listen. Mario is right." Claire turned to Alberto. "*Isn't* he right, Alberto?" Alberto nodded his head.

There were tears in his eyes and he reached down and kissed Mario on the forehead.

Tia sank back in her chair and put her head in her hands. Just then, Marion woke up and started crying. "Go to the bedroom and nurse her, Tia," Jimmy urged. "Just trust us to carry on. We won't make any life altering decisions without your approval, I promise."

After Tia left, the room buzzed with various conversations as the group present speculated on how this entirely different scenario could work.

"If we did this, when would Mr. Hendricks be willing to leave?" Claire asked Mario. Everyone fell silent and turned to listen to what Mario had to say.

"I have been telling him all about what has been happening to nonna and about those people getting murdered in the hospital. Last night when I said I was going over to my friends to study for a test I really went there." He looked at Jimmy guiltily. "Well, you *know* how mom is. I didn't dare even mention it to her until I had everything worked out with Mr. Hendricks. She'd have just told me not to interfere."

Jimmy nodded his head, reached for Mario's hand and pulled him down beside him on the sofa, placing his arm around him. He could feel Mario still trembling and decided he'd have to have a firm word with Tia about her temper and about treating Mario age appropriately. Even though the appropriate age would be about thirty.

"Tell us everything, son," he said gently.

"Well, when I told him how urgent it was, he said if we just agreed to buy the house and the furniture as is, he could move out as soon as he could get his stuff together, maybe in a week."

Mario turned to his grandfather then and said, "I explained that you could not pay him until you sold your house in Wetaskiwin, nonno. But he told me there's something called bridge financing. That means you can borrow the money from the bank and pay it back when you sell your house."

Amanda had been listening quietly up to this point and now she asked, "What about the price? If he knows we really want the house, he might ask more than it's worth."

"No, I discussed that with him. I explained that nonno and nonna were really nice people and not very rich and he shouldn't try to take advantage of them. I said he needed to have a property assessment done by a professional and we would split the cost. That's because I remember what Aunty Claire said when you were buying the house across the street." Mario gulped and looked at Jimmy.

"You did right, son," he said, ruffling his hair. "And has he arranged for this assessment."

"Well, he called and the man has tentatively arranged to come out on Thursday—day after tomorrow—but he's waiting to hear back from you, nonno, before setting up the appointment."

"It's 8 o'clock. Do you think he would let us see the house, now?" Jimmy asked.

"Yes. I told him about the meeting tonight and he said you could come over anytime before nine."

Jimmy glanced at the others and he saw that they were all interested in following up on this idea. "Can you phone him, Mario, and ask if we can come over now? Tell him that there are quite a few of us but I'll bring him your mother's cake."

Mario picked up the phone just as Tia emerged from the bedroom carrying Marion. "What about my cake?"

Jimmy motioned to Mario to carry on and then led Tia back to the bedroom so they could speak in private. They were gone ten minutes and the rest of the group listened nervously. Occasionally they heard Tia's raised voice and Jimmy's soothing responses. Once in awhile they heard his voice rise as well and the group was feeling exceedingly nervous when they finally emerged from the bedroom.

Jimmy was carrying the baby and he handed her over to Amanda. "Amanda, I'm sure you'd like to see the house, too, but can I ask you to stay here with Marion, please?" Amanda smiled and nodded her head.

"I think she'll probably need changing one last time and then she should be ready for sleep soon. She got a little upset by all the 'action' but I'm sure you have ways to calm her down."

"I'll practice my singing voice on her," Amanda grinned. "If nothing else, she'll go to sleep just to shut me out." The rest of the group laughed and the tension was broken.

Mr. Hendricks looked somewhat overwhelmed when he opened his door to find eight adults and one smallish boy crowded on his doorstep and lining the front steps. He invited them in and when they all awkwardly bent over to remove their shoes in his small entrance hall, he just shook his head and told them to keep them on.

The house was very similar in size and design to Jimmy and Tia's house next door and most of the group was satisfied with a quick walk through after which Mr. Hendricks invited them to sit down in his living room where he'd set out extra chairs. He brought out some coffee he'd made once he knew they were coming and also provided a plate of tasty Costco ginger snaps. An old friend had bought him a large bag because he knew they were his favorite.

While Tia busily sliced her *Company's Coming* cake book Crumb Cake, Alvin Hendricks talked to them about the many years he'd spent in the house and some of his favorite memories there. He mentioned the garden he'd put in their large back yard because his wife was so fond of gardening and how meticulously she had maintained it until she became too ill to work on it any longer. He had tried to keep it up for her sake when she was still alive but after she died, he just didn't have the heart for it and it had fallen into decay.

Alberto mentioned then that he too enjoyed gardening and if they bought the house, he planned to get it all fixed up. Alvin smiled for the first time and said, "It would help me a lot to know that somebody was loving Marie's garden the way she did and looking after it. I feel like I have betrayed her memory by letting it go." There were tears in his eyes when he said this.

This was too much for Mario who was very softhearted. He went over to Mr. Hendricks and awkwardly clasped his arms around him. "You can come back and visit any time you like and you can even stay here in the house." He looked pleadingly at Alberto when he said this.

Alberto nodded his head in agreement. "Yes, you are welcome to stay here when you visit. I would enjoy your company and showing you what I had done with the garden. And if Marisa gets better, she would want you to be here, too."

"*When* she gets better, not *if*," Jimmy remonstrated.

Alvin and Alberto talked of many things then and found they had a lot in common but some separate strong interests as well. Alberto liked art and enjoyed sharing it with Mario. On the coming Saturday, they were already planning to go the Art Gallery of Alberta together to see a visiting exhibition of Italian Arte Povera—an art form originating in Italy in the 1960's that makes use of common objects as a way of undermining the growing use of art as a form of commerce.

Alvin, not to be outdone, mentioned that he and Mario had spent time on several occasions listening to records from his extensive jazz collection, his own particular interest, and Mario had especially liked the ones featuring Miles Davis and Sarah Vaughn. Mario nodded his head in agreement, all the time looking nervously back and forth between the two of them.

The rest of the group was wise enough to just sit back and listen. Dan hadn't joined them because he was busy exploring the house in depth, taking various measurements and mentally making his plans. From what he could tell, the house appeared structurally sound with no evidence of basement leakage. Both the plumbing and the wiring appeared to be in good condition and he could tell that this was a home in which the owners had taken pride and attended to basic upkeep.

Back in the living room, it appeared that the conversation between Alvin and Alberto was winding down and turning to practical details involving the whole group. Alvin explained to them that he and Mario had already discussed financial issues at some length and it soon became quite clear that Alvin only wanted a fair price for his house, less than it would have cost to go through a realtor and even some further concession for quick occupancy.

"It will make it much easier for me to leave knowing that somebody will be buying the house who will appreciate it and keep up Marie's garden," he explained. "And now that I've come to terms with leaving, the sooner I go, the better." He had contacted the property inspector after their earlier phone call and the man had agreed to come out the very next day since he'd had a cancellation. As soon as his report was ready, Alvin and Alberto would negotiate the final price.

The group trouped out then and at the door Alvin gave Mario a spontaneous hug. "You are quite the young man," he said huskily. "I wish I had a grandson like you. *My* grandson has what they call a learning disability and he's not so quick on the uptake—but he *is* a nice boy."

Claire perked up when she heard this and opened her mouth to comment, but Tia anticipated what would be coming next and jabbed her in the ribs somewhat harder than necessary. She was still feeling unsettled and rather embarrassed by her earlier behavior and it felt good to let some of the tension out.

Back at the house everyone tried to talk at once, explaining to Amanda what had taken place and providing their various impressions on the situation. Finally, Dan asked for the floor, stating that he and Claire had to leave soon to relieve the sitter. He described the state of the house and sketched out a few suggestions for how it could be modified to meet Marisa's needs. They spent several minutes considering the timeline and then Claire and Dan left.

When the door finally closed behind the rest of the group, Tia wanted to talk some more about the house but Jimmy just held up his hand. Mario had gone off to bed and he led Tia into the living room and sat down beside her on the sofa. "I'm not going to discuss the house any further until we talk about what happened tonight," he said to Tia.

Tia looked at him belligerently. "He's *my* son and I don't want him growing up spoilt and entitled like his father."

Jimmy said nothing for a moment, collecting his thoughts—but he felt like he'd been punched in the stomach. Finally, he spoke, careful to keep his tone mild because he knew how touchy Tia was on this subject. "Mario is no longer only *your* son. He is *our* son. If you recall, I am now legally his father. Furthermore, Mario and I have connected at a deep level and I consider myself morally and emotionally his father as well. And I do not want *my* son treated the way you treated him tonight, *particularly* in front of other people. I do not want to see him embarrassed and discounted for no good reason. He was only trying to do his best for his grandmother—about whom he is every bit as concerned as *you* are. And, as it happens, he's done very well by her with his negotiations and he deserves high praise for his efforts, not criticism."

Tia said nothing in response but merely closed her eyes and wept silently. Jimmy didn't move to comfort her. He felt that this issue was far too important to sweep to one side and he needed to stand his ground. Finally, she spoke. "I just don't want him to be like his biological father."

"He is *not*. You have made *sure* of that. But now you are in danger of going too far and undermining his self-confidence, the self-confidence he needs to get through life successfully. I want you to start respecting him more and trusting him more. He is a *good boy!*"

They heard a noise at the living room doorway then and saw Alberto standing there. "Sorry," he said. "I couldn't sleep and I thought I would warm some milk. I couldn't help overhearing. Jimmy is right, Tia. You are too hard on Mario sometimes."

Tia sat motionless and Jimmy put his arm around her. "Thanks, Alberto," he said. "I know you are very close to Mario and understand him very well." Turning to Tia, he said, "It's time for us to go to bed. Marion will be up soon so we better get some sleep." But his real agenda was that he didn't want Tia to feel ganged up on—and he *certainly* didn't want to have to tell Alberto to butt out.

Chapter 18: A Close Call

Mila Thorquist yawned. It was four in the morning and her shift wouldn't be over for another three hours. *Time for another bathroom break,* she thought. She left the nursing station and, as was her habit, Mila stopped briefly as she passed each door on her way to the staff washroom that happened to be just inside the adjoining unit. At the third door, she hesitated before moving on. Had she seen movement? Everyone was on high alert these days so it was probably just her imagination.

Mila slowly opened the door so as not to wake the woman sleeping in the first bed and gasped in horror. Someone she didn't know was standing over the patient, holding a pillow. In another moment, she realized it must be one of the practical nurses from the adjoining unit since she was wearing a nurse's uniform. "What are you *doing*?" Mila whispered hoarsely.

The other nurse didn't reply but carefully arranged the pillow under Marisa's head before walking quickly out of the room. "Her pillow had slipped out onto the floor and I was just putting it back," she said curtly to Mila and then headed towards the far end of the other unit without waiting for a response. Mila walked on to the washroom thinking she mustn't be so jumpy. Night shifts could make you imagine all kinds of odd things, especially in the early morning hours. She must keep control of herself.

Claire visited Marisa early the next morning, just after eight. Oddly, she was still asleep, something Claire hadn't seen in her early morning visits for a couple of weeks now. Her roommate, however, was wide awake and enjoying her breakfast. "Good morning, Mrs. Barton. How are you today?"

Mrs. Barton was a heavy lady who enjoyed her food and enjoyed being looked after by others. She was also fond of a good gossip. "I'm a bit tired this morning. There was a little excitement in here last night."

"O-o-h?" Claire asked, instantly on the alert. Mrs. Barton told her what had happened and Claire asked who the nurse was.

"Don't know. Haven't seen her before. Of course, I usually sleep pretty soundly at night." Claire was about to ask for further details, a physical description, but just then Marisa made some rustling sounds and it was clear she was waking up.

"How *are* you this morning?" she asked Marisa, anxiously.

"Drowsy. Funny dream—like choking," Marisa responded slowly in slurred words.

Claire quickly turned back to Mrs. Barton who had opened her mouth to say something, but Claire shook her head to indicate that she was not to tell Marisa what had happened. She turned the bed light on and saw that Marisa's breakfast tray was already on her table. "Well, have some breakfast, Marisa, and maybe you'll feel better."

Claire cut her visit short and went to the unit desk to ask the nurse there if she'd heard what had happened. "*Nothing* happened," was the curt reply. "Mrs. Barton has an active *imagination*!" Claire left, knowing it was no use to push any further. She then went to the second unit to ask the name of the nurse who'd been on duty the night before. But even after she'd explained why she wanted that information, she was stone walled. "We don't give out staff names for security reasons," she was told.

"Humph, *some security*!" Claire muttered, and stomped off.

After arriving at the Co-op a few minutes late, she advised Roscoe to hurry up with his morning routine as they were scheduled to visit the Space Science Centre for the 11 o'clock Imax show about Madagascar monkeys. While she waited for him, Claire called Jimmy at work. Normally she would have talked to Tia but she didn't want to upset her.

"Wow!" was all Jimmy could think to say. "That's *scary!*"

"Yes," Claire replied, "but what are we going to *do* about it?"

"Well, Alvin brought over the house assessment this morning, and Alberto and Dan are meeting with him tonight to settle the deal. Alvin says he hopes to be out of there by the weekend."

"That's *great!*" Claire said. "But it's still going to take time to do the renovations and something could happen to Marisa any day. Look what happened last night! We need to take her out of there right now and just cope somehow until we get things organized."

"You don't absolutely know that that was anything," Jimmy pointed out. "And even if it was, the fact that this nurse was almost caught in the act makes it unlikely she'd try again with Marisa. That other nurse would be sure to report her if something happened."

Claire gritted her teeth. *Men's minds!* she thought

"And don't say anything to Tia. You know how she worries," Jimmy added.

The rest of the morning passed normally. Claire and Roscoe both enjoyed the Imax show and then went out for lunch at a nearby Boston Pizza. Roscoe ate his pineapple pizza with relish but Claire only picked away at her lasagna.

"Wha wong, Claih? You not eat."

Claire looked at Roscoe. He was her client and she was his boss in the work setting and she shouldn't blur those boundaries. But Roscoe was easy to talk to. He didn't judge her when she let her thoughts roam. And she couldn't talk to Tia about this, the one person she really needed to talk to. It would be too upsetting for her. Talking to Jimmy had not been much help and talking to Dan would be no better. He'd just tell her to stop trying to save the world or something equally irritating.

Roscoe continued to look steadily at Claire, waiting for her to respond and before she knew it, Claire found herself pouring out all her confused thoughts and fears about Marisa to him. When she finally wound down, Roscoe remained silent for a full minute. He hadn't been able to follow everything Claire had said. In point of fact, even the most mentally vigorous person would've had some difficulty because of Claire's tendency to talk in circles, one thought leading to another. But finally, Roscoe responded to what he considered to be the most salient points.

"You say Mawisa in danger at night. All those people killed at night and we go in the day to visit Mawisa, but that not help too much."

"That's right, Roscoe. I'm afraid that is right."

"And Mawisa can't come here because she can't use our staff? Because govment pay for us but not Mawisa?"

"That is exactly the problem, Roscoe".

"Then *I* pay for Mawisa's staff," Roscoe concluded triumphantly.

"No, Roscoe. You *can't*."

"Why? I have the money. Daisuke say the westaurant do well now. He say that because of *you,* Claih. And you hep me when that Wu Heng try to kill me. Wemembah? I go to Vancouvah, and then Mexico, and then you and Tia find Wu Heng and you both get huht just to protect me and now I can't hep you. *Why?*"

Claire had no answer for Roscoe because he was right. His reasoning was utterly sound. In fact, it was far sounder than many without his mental challenges. *What can I say back to him?* Claire asked herself. *That I have to ask his parents who are his guardians and trustees? Do I tell him that his mother is mean with money and not anxious to share Roscoe's good fortune with any of the rest of us? And how would that make Roscoe feel?*

Roscoe was silent, still waiting for an answer, and Claire felt she had to say something. "That's a very generous offer, Roscoe. I'm sure that Tia and Jimmy and Mario and Alberto and Marisa will be very grateful when I tell them. But you know that your parents have control over your money and they may not agree. However, even if they don't, we will all be very grateful to you for offering. I guess you will have to discuss it with them and see what they say."

"Daisuke hep me," Roscoe said. "Daisuke unnerstan."

Claire *knew* that. She had often thought that it was too bad Daisuke was not Roscoe's parent or guardian. He was so much more in tune with him than his parents. "You can try, Roscoe," Claire responded. "If you succeed, it would be a really helpful short-term solution but it would not help in the long run. Your restaurant makes *some* money but not enough to hire the staff Marisa will need on a long-term basis. But to be able to get her out of there right now would be wonderful—before something happens."

"I talk to Daisuke this aftanoon," Roscoe said. He was scheduled to work in the restaurant as cashier and they had to leave shortly.

"Okay, you do that," Claire said, and got up to leave. But just then her cell phone rang.

"Claire? It's Hilda. I was wondering if I could visit you. Job and I went to visit Marisa just now and something was not right."

"I will be free at two this afternoon, Hilda. I can meet you at the restaurant if that's okay."

When Hilda arrived at the restaurant, she had Job with her. Claire gulped but didn't let on her concern and led Hilda and Job to a table in the back corner away from direct site of the entrance. She hoped no food inspector would decide to come in at that moment but if he or she did, Claire would just tell them that Job was a therapy dog. Certainly, Hilda got that look on her face at times that suggested she *did* need a therapy dog.

Once their coffee arrived, Claire asked, "What happened, Hilda?"

"When we got to the hospital, an ambulance was just pulling out and it had the siren on. But I didn't think much about it. I thought maybe somebody had had a heart attack or something. But then, when we got to Marisa's room, I saw there were two paramedics in there."

"Whose bed?" Claire interrupted, hardly daring to breathe.

"They were talking to that other lady and examining an oxygen cylinder—and then that policeman came, that McCoy. He asked her who'd brought the cylinder in and I heard her say a nurse—a nurse with red hair. And then some more police arrived and they shooed me away so I couldn't hear any more."

"What about Marisa? What was happening to her all this time?"

"She wasn't there. I thought they must have moved her. Remember you told me they tried to move her before when her roommate was killed."

"Was her bed there?" Claire asked, her heart pounding.

"Y-e-s," Hilda replied slowly, considering that for the first time. "Perhaps…"

But Claire wasn't listening. She was searching for her phone to call Tia but just then it rang. When she picked it up, Tia blurted, "La mamma is in the Grey Nuns Hospital. Somebody tried to murder her with an overdose of anesthetic!"

"I was just calling you. Hilda is here. She was there and she came to tell me."

"Go, Claire. I can't!" Tia sobbed. "Marion is sleeping and Amanda is not home."

"I'm on my way," Claire said tersely. "I'll call you as soon as I know something."

"I could come with you?" Hilda offered.

"No! Go to Tia. Take Job!" and Claire rushed back to see Daisuke and tell him that he was responsible for Roscoe because she had to leave.

"Call Tom at the Co-op at four. He can come and pick him up," she told him—and then rushed out of the restaurant.

So much for Jimmy's clever theories! Claire muttered to herself, driving as fast as she could without attracting unwanted attention from any lurking police car. *I should have followed my instincts. I always go wrong when I don't follow my instincts.*

At the Grey Nuns, the same hospital Claire and Hazel had gone to during Hazel's anaphylaxis scare, Claire found a fairly convenient parking space, dropped as much change as she had in her purse into the meter and rushed in to the admissions desk. She asked for Marisa and, at first, the clerk couldn't find her in the computer. A deeper search revealed that she was actually in the intensive care unit and no visitors were allowed. "I need to speak to her doctor!" Claire demanded.

"Are you a relative?"

"No. I'm a close family friend and I'm here on behalf of her daughter, Tiziana Elves. You can call her if you like. I have the number." Claire was shifting from one foot to the other, obviously agitated and the clerk looked at her closely.

Finally, the clerk said, "I'll call the ICU and see what they have to say."

She did so, listened, raised her eyebrows, hung up the phone and said to Claire. "Well, she's out of the ICU and in the recovery room where they can keep a close eye on her. The nurse said you can come up and see her briefly and she can update you on her condition. She's calling your friend to confirm. As you heard, I gave her the number. They were happy to have it as apparently she came with no contact information. I guess the ambulance people rushed her out pretty fast."

Claire's heart jumped when she heard this. *It must have been a really close call. What would the fall-out be? Would it precipitate another stroke? Would Marisa have more brain damage?* She had much to ask the nurse when she saw her. But the first thing Claire needed to do was to check in on Marisa.

Marisa appeared to be in a deep sleep, her lungs moving up and down slowly. She was intubated and had an oxygen monitor on. A drip was attached to her left arm above the elbow. The monitor by her bedside indicated that blood pressure and pulse were low and brain wave activity was minimal indicating a state of deep unconsciousness.

The first thing Claire asked when she met up with the nurse a few minutes later, was "What was in that canister?"

The nurse was taken aback and not sure she should answer, but Claire continued to glare at her fiercely. Finally she replied, "Your friend was administered an opioid anesthetic. That's why she's intubated. In high doses such as she received, it suppresses lung function."

"Why did this happen. Why weren't we told?"

"We don't know who did it. A nurse did it—or somebody dressed as a nurse—is all we know, and we only know that because of her roommate, a Mrs. Barton. The woman came into the room when your friend was sleeping and placed a mask over her nose attached to a tank of this anesthetic/oxygen mix. Then she left and nobody else saw her coming or going."

"Did Mrs. Barton call for help right away?"

"No. She thought it was part of your friend's treatment and just carried on reading her Bible. She reported that your friend had been very restless and upset that morning so Mrs. Barton thought they were just giving her something to calm her down. It was only when she heard Marisa's breathing slowing right down that she got concerned and rang for the nurse—who apparently did not come right away. When the paramedics asked her about the delay, she explained that Mrs. Barton tends to be very demanding so they don't respond quickly. That's the story—all we could get from the paramedics who brought Marisa in."

"Is Marisa going to recover fully? Will there be any complications?"

"We don't know yet. This particular anesthetic doesn't tend to cause long-term organ damage. If her lungs regain their full function, she should be physically all right. Cognitively, we're not sure yet."

"How long will she need to stay here?"

"The doctors will want to keep a close eye on her for a couple of days. Then if everything is okay she should be able to be returned to the extended care hospital."

"She's *not* going back there!" Claire said harshly. "Who do I have to talk to make sure that does not happen?"

"Her next of kin will have to come in to make those arrangements. Otherwise we are legally obligated to send her back there, given that she's unable to speak for herself at this point."

"Her husband, Alberto, will be here this evening. Can he sign then or are there only certain hours?"

"He can sign any time but tell him to bring id—his and hers—and a copy of their marriage certificate or health care cards to validate the legality of their relationship."

Chapter 19: Somehow, Claire Makes It Work

Claire drove straight back to Tia's home, alternately fuming and thinking. By the time she arrived, she had the beginnings of a plan. Tia and Jimmy were predictably horrified when they heard the story. Tia had called to tell him Marisa was in the hospital and he'd come home as soon as he could to be with her.

When she finished, Claire turned to Jimmy and said angrily, "I should have followed my instincts and not listened to you!"

"What's she talking about, Jimmy?"

He told Tia then about the apparent previous attack and, as he was expecting, she lashed out at him.

Claire, in turn, snarled at Tia and inadvertently came to Jimmy's defense. "We have both been doing our best to look after Marisa and protect you from getting upset but you haven't been much help, acting all vulnerable all the time. How about if you just suck it up and we focus on finding a way to keep Marisa out of that damned extended care hospital."

Tia and Jimmy both sat there in shocked silence. Claire *never* swore. It was a point of honor with her. Tia clasped Jimmy's hand and turned to Claire. "Let's get to work."

But just then Mario came in from school and wanted to know what was happening. At the same time, Marion woke up from her afternoon nap. Tia, with a crispness and efficiency that spoke of the old Tia, turned to him and said, "Nonna's in the hospital but she should be okay. We're busy trying to work some things out. Would you be able to look after your sister for a while? There's a bottle of breast milk in the fridge and you know where the clean diapers and baby wipes are."

"I'm on it!" he said. "Don't worry, mamma. Take all the time you need." Mario walked proudly toward Marion's bedroom. Nonna had just begun to teach him how to care for Marion before her stroke and she had trusted him. But his mother always resisted getting him involved. *Part of her controlling nature,* he thought to himself. He wondered what had happened to nonna but knew better than to ask right now. He would be told in due course. Right now he was going to focus on keeping Marion happy and well cared for.

Mario wanted to prove to his mother that he could do it and she didn't have to worry. He wanted his parents to go out alone together more and relax. The situation was entirely too tense at home these days. If they knew he was always there and could handle things they could just go out spontaneously when they had the energy and felt like it. That would be good for them and ultimately good for him and Marion. Besides, he loved his sister and resented the fact that his mother was always hovering over her when she was home and leaving no space for him to get involved.

Mario wished nonna were here. She always understood him. And he didn't even have the close, easy relationship with nonno that he used to have before nonna got sick. Nonno was always looking sad and worried and he hardly talked anymore. Maybe on Saturday when they went to the art gallery together they would get close again.

Back in the living room, Claire was laying out her plan. "Marisa has been more responsive lately, especially early in the morning when she first wakes up. You're never there then, Tia, so you don't know." Tia nodded her head and the tears started to come.

"Cut it out!" Claire snarled. "This is the time for action, not guilt and regret. I have a plan. Just stop blubbering and listen!" She turned to Jimmy then and said curtly, "And don't *you* start rolling your eyes and hurrying me up. I'll tell it to you in my own way." But just then Marion started to fuss again and Tia rose hurriedly to go to her.

"Sit down!" Claire and Jimmy shouted together. "Mario can handle it," Jimmy added. "You never give him enough credit and that stops *now!*"

Claire had never heard Jimmy speak so assertively about Mario before and was secretly thrilled. But she also recognized how it reflected the high stress level they were all experiencing. *It just cannot go on, not just for Marisa's sake, but for all our sakes. Anything is better than this.*

"Continue, Claire," Jimmy said. "I promise to shut up." Tia nodded her head in agreement.

"I've already talked to Marisa several times about getting out of the hospital. I've told her about our plans to date, about the house, about using Mavis' tub for the time being, about spending time over there with me and Roscoe. She would be okay with all of that."

"There's no problem from her end, then," Jimmy said.

"There *is* a problem," Claire said. "She doesn't want to be a burden and she's squeamish about having her personal needs met by family members. Any of us would feel the same way when you really think about it."

"Well, what choice do we have?" Tia asked, noting that Mario was now sitting in a comfortable chair in the adjoining family room giving Marion her bottle.

"If you want to get people to help, you have to show them what's in it for them and if you can kill two birds with one stone, it makes life go a little smoother." Both Tia and Jimmy involuntarily rolled their eyes at this portentous statement. It was so typically Claire—both clichéd and hokey. And yet, her peculiar lines of reasoning and her funny way of expressing them often led to startlingly effective results.

Claire didn't see the eye rolls because when she got into this particular space she was really talking to herself. "We all know that Hilda is not herself. She's fumbling around looking for a way forward. She needs something to grab onto. She needs to feel useful and needed." Claire looked at them then and Tia and Jimmy both nodded dutifully.

Claire went on then, half ruminating, half-talking. "You know I've been wanting to establish a day program for Mavis at home for some time. I don't feel she gets much out of the setting she's in now. But the trouble is that I don't want to place her in a cocoon interacting with only me or another assistant all day long." Again, her listeners nodded dutifully. In the family room, Mario was listening, too –and smirking. He understood Claire better than most of them, having a pretty complicated mind himself.

"Alberto is another problem," Claire went on. "Where is he, anyway?"

"A friend picked him up today to help him make salami. Alberto looked happier than I've seen him look since before Marisa's stroke," Jimmy explained. "He doesn't know yet about what happened to Marisa today."

"Good," Claire said briskly. "He needs his own life. Moving him into the city and turning him into a care provider for Marisa would not be the right thing to do."

Tia had had enough. Marion was fussing again and she just knew that Mario didn't know how to burp her properly. She jumped up. "Where are you going with all this, Claire? Could you please get to the point? I have to get supper going."

Claire looked at her reproachfully and stood up. She said huffily, "Here it is, assuming you agree—since you have the authority but not the plan." Tia nodded her head meekly, conceding the argument. "In two days or so, we get Marisa out of the hospital. We move her in across the street for the time being. That house belongs to Mavis, Roscoe and Bill. You are guardians for two of them and I'm pretty sure Daisuke will be able to bring Roscoe's parents around." She told them then of Roscoe's offer. "If his parent's agree, we try to hire somebody part-time and get Hilda to help out some of the time. Hilda and I can attend to Marisa's personal needs. I think Marisa can handle that. I'm not family. I think Hilda can handle that and actually benefit from it, from having some focus in her life. Also, she may be an accountant but apart from having some mathematical skill she's not a particularly sophisticated or deep-thinking person. She can even bring the dog if she wants. She has trouble finding places she can bring Job. It's one of her frustrations."

Claire stopped to take a breath and further collect her thoughts and Tia took the opportunity to interject. "That might work right now but it can't work in the long term. What about that?"

"I'm just getting to that," Claire said. "I've asked Dan to work out a plan for basement development in the new house. As you know, it's already partially walled in and there's actually room for two bedrooms, a large kitchen/dining/living area and even a tiny third bedroom or den down there. It could house a small family. There are many new refugees flooding into the city because of the disgusting state the world is in right now. We'll advertise and I bet we won't have any problem finding a suitable couple with maybe one or two young children to live there rent-free in return for helping out with Marisa. Alberto can have a bell upstairs and if he needs help with her during the night, one or both of them can go up. We'll build in a ceiling lift, of course."

Jimmy and Tia were both blinking rapidly by this time trying to follow Claire's line of thought. But Tia knew her better and jumped in. "What about days?"

"Well, that's just it. Don't you see?" They both shook their heads.

Alberto is going to become a volunteer for Bill, walk him back and forth to the restaurant, for example. And Marisa is going to become a volunteer for Mavis, reading to her and working on simple rehabilitation exercises together, which Marisa is going to need in order to regain function. So they will both be spending part of their day at the house. "Oh, and that man who's going to live with Alberto and Marisa will be responsible for shoveling the walks and mowing the lawn if the time comes that Alberto can't manage." Claire turned to Jimmy. "I'm sure you don't want it all to fall on you, Jimmy?"

Jimmy just looked at Claire stunned. "This is a beautiful castle in the sand you're building, Claire—but what if it all falls apart?"

"Well, it *will* with that attitude. Just trust me, okay? I've only had time to give you a rough outline. There are other details I'm in the process of working out. I'm going home now. Do I have your approval to move ahead or *not*?"

Tia and Jimmy looked at Claire and then at each other. This was Claire at her most obnoxious and most endearing: bossing, creating and taking over.

Mario walked into the room at that point, holding baby Marion. He handed her to his mother and said, "Just agree. You know Aunty Claire will do it right." Jimmy looked once more at Tia and then turned to Claire. "Just carry on," he said. "Tell us what you need us to do." He hesitated for a moment and then walked over to her and put his arms around her. "And thanks," he said huskily.

Claire nodded her head mutely, almost in tears herself. The relationship between her and Jimmy had always been somewhat fraught. It felt very good to be so totally trusted by him. She headed for the door and said, "I'll be in touch and keep you updated. I'll email you a list of what *you* need to do. First thing is to get to that extended care hospital and collect Marisa's purse—*and* her valuables. Then get Alberto and all necessary id to the Grey Nuns tonight so he can sign the paper stating that Marisa is *not* to return to that hospital and that he will be taking personal responsibility for her as next of kin. Bye." And with that, Claire was out the door.

The next two days passed in a blur. Marisa was continuing to recover from the overdose of anesthesia and it looked at this point like there would be no long-term complications. Tia had taken time off from her hospital position. They could hardly object, given what had happened to her mother. She'd taken the opportunity to remove all her mother's possessions from the hospital and to inform them that Marisa would not be returning. Tia stressed that under the circumstances, they should return the remainder of the monthly fee for the unused days and again the administration saw no choice but to comply.

Alberto closed the deal on the house for less than expected and for less than the bridge funding he'd been able to negotiate on his property in Wetaskiwin. Thus there was enough money available to go ahead with the basement renovations. Dan and Jimmy lost no time in ordering the necessary supplies and having them delivered, and Alvin gave them permission to get started on the basement even before he'd completely moved out. With too much time on his hands in the three years since his wife had passed away, he had combed through the basement, eliminating much of the detritus collected in 30 years of living there. The rest, Jimmy and Dan managed to move up to the living room and Alvin was in the process of going through it to decide what to take with him, what to sell and what to give away. One evening he held a little farewell party for the few friends he had left in the area and the next morning Jimmy noticed that most of it was gone.

Jimmy, Fuji and Randy's two sons who were currently finished with their university year set to work framing and insulating the unfinished part of the basement but they left the end facing the back yard alone. Dan had arranged for professional contractors to rip out a window well and part of the wall so they could build a basement walkout that would also function as a secondary fire escape.

Meanwhile, Fuji's wife, Yuni, and his daughter-in-law, Hura, had visited the new house to measure for new curtains and purchase the necessary material in colors complementary to the wall paint colors chosen by Dan and Alberto. Two of Marisa's Italian friends then took the material home with them to make up the curtains for the downstairs as well as new curtains for several of the upstairs rooms where the existing ones were badly faded or worn. Alvin reminded them that he was leaving most of his furniture behind and since Alberto would be bringing some furniture from the house in Wetaskiwin as well they wouldn't need much extra to furnish the suite.

Tia and Jimmy went over to check on the progress every evening, leaving Marion with Mario, a process with which Tia had now become quite comfortable. They marveled at how quickly things were coming together and what magic a community could perform. "Claire was right," Jimmy said softly. "I never quite believe she can pull it off when she comes up with one of her wild schemes—and somehow she always does."

"She's gone through a lot because of Jessie and all along the way it's just seemed to make her more and more determined. I feel privileged to call her my friend," Tia said with a catch in her voice.

Jimmy put his arm around her. "It's going to be alright," he said.

Meanwhile, Claire had been in close consultation with Hilda and, not surprisingly, Hilda had initially resisted Claire's idea for her to become a volunteer care provider for Marisa. "I'm an accountant. I'm not going to become anybody's servant. What did I go to school for?" she asked Claire.

"You *were* an accountant," Claire had responded in exasperation, feeling that she didn't have the time to pussyfoot around on the issue. "Now you're in free fall. You don't know *where* you're going or *what* you're going to do. You need an anchor—and I'm not exactly talking about the rest of your life. But this can help for now. You will have company and a purpose. You need those to help with your healing." And she added somewhat belligerently, "Are you going to pretend you *don't* need to heal?" And, as a final kicker, Claire added, "And what do you think your mother would want you to do in this situation, given all we've done for Bill and Jimmy's responsibility as Bill's guardian?"

Claire had to meet with Hilda three different times before she could even get her to go to the house but when she finally did, what really convinced Hilda was Mavis! For some reason they clicked. Mavis couldn't talk and in Hilda's present state, that was a good thing. That was partly the reason Hilda had connected so strongly with Job. The very first time Hilda had visited the house and was introduced to Mavis, Mavis just looked at her and then spontaneously reached out and touched her hand. After that, Hilda was hooked, particularly when she was told that she could bring Job with her.

Meanwhile, Claire and Roscoe and Daisuke had been talking. His parents had agreed, under a certain amount of pressure from Daisuke to which neither Claire nor Roscoe were privy, that some of the restaurant profits could be used to provide a part-time care provider for Marisa for up to three months. Claire assured them that she was hoping the time would be much less than that depending on when the basement suite was ready and they could find a suitable family.

With all the adventures happening at the hospital, neither Claire nor Tia had had much time or energy to focus on the news but a huge fire in Fort McMurray in May that had burned down part of the city was on everybody's mind. Edmonton was now full of refugees, and appeals for support were everywhere. Dan and Jimmy and Alberto all made trips to the bank to contribute financially, funds that were then matched by the province, the federal government and even the bank. Everyone was pulling together in this time of crisis and the alternately dazed and grateful looks on the faces of the fire refugees at the Northlands Centre were heartbreaking.

In the few spare moments they had, Tia and Claire scoured their homes for extra clothes and household supplies to help people get re-established. Claire had suggested to Hilda that she might like to do the same, but Hilda just looked at her with those glassy eyes so characteristic of her since the car accident. Claire knew that Hilda was just not capable of crawling out of the emotional swamp she was in far enough to empathize with others so she didn't push it.

Back at the restaurant, Roscoe was also concerned with the refugee problem and he'd asked Daisuke to take him to the bank and co-sign for him so he could contribute from the small personal account his parents had set up for him. But what bothered him even more was a man who came into the restaurant occasionally for coffee. Roscoe was a good listener and the man, whose first name was Mohammed, told Roscoe his story.

He and his wife, Noor, and 6-year old daughter, Leila, were refugees from a small town in Syria. He was a mechanic and his wife was a trained nurse who had worked in the hospital there until it was bombed. They had escaped when their town was invaded and destroyed by ISIL and ended up in a refugee camp in Jordan. It had become like a little town with people trying to pull together and help each other. Mohammed had been able to help out with some mechanical work and his wife had worked as a volunteer nurse for Doctors Without Borders in the health center that had been set up there. Then they found out that they'd been chosen to come to Canada as part of the Syrian refugee initiative and 18 months after arriving at the camp they left for Edmonton, Alberta, where they'd been assigned. Because Mohammed had been a maintenance specialist for heavy equipment at an oil field in Syria prior to the war, he had been able to get work in Fort McMurray and set up his family in a small but nice apartment in the Beacon Hill area.

Mohammed had been at work at the camp with their only car when the fire struck Fort McMurray so suddenly and savagely that his wife just had time to grab the essentials and their passports before being evacuated with her daughter. Mohammed had later joined them at the refugee center in Edmonton. They soon found out that the building their apartment was in had burnt to the ground along with most of the Beacon Hill district of Fort McMurray. And Mohammed's oil camp was the one oil camp that had been destroyed. There was absolutely nothing left for them to return to. After all they'd been through and all they'd lost and left behind in Syria, they now had even less than when they'd arrived in Canada.

Claire heard the story from Roscoe and one day she was in the restaurant when Mohammed came in with his wife, Noor and daughter, Leila. She found out that the Red Cross had recently put them up in a neighborhood hotel and Leila was now attending a nearby elementary school. Claire visited with them for quite some time and found them to be intelligent, energetic people who wanted to work and get ahead in life. An idea was forming in her head and she excused herself to go to the washroom but once there she called Tia. Tia agreed to her plan and Claire returned to the table to invite them to supper at Tia's home.

One of the many thoughts that had been swarming around in Claire's mind was a fear of bed bugs that might invade Alberto's and Marisa's new home if, by bad luck, they moved in a family who'd been exposed to bedbugs in their previous rental accommodation. Terrible as the fire was, it effectively eliminated the bed bug threat in this case and Claire saw that as another reason for moving ahead with the couple instead of advertising.

Another of Claire's concerns was that Alberto and Marisa—older and set in their ways—could be distressed if inundated by too many exotic cooking smells from their tenants. Hence she'd insisted that Dan search out through his contacts a heavy duty industrial kitchen fan and design the new downstairs kitchen in such a way that the stove fan could be directly vented outside. Claire's theory was that any potential irritant that could be anticipated and eliminated in advance would increase the likelihood of success of the whole venture.

Another concern was cleanliness. Claire noted that Mohammed and his wife and daughter all looked neat and clean and that his wife took their daughter to the washroom to wash her hands before eating the plate of chips she'd been allowed to order as a special treat. She talked to the woman and found out that she'd been a nurse in Syria and was hoping to eventually take the further training in Edmonton necessary to qualify as a registered nurse in Alberta but that dream was likely some years down the road. *Yes, this could work,* Claire thought but didn't express her idea out loud.

Yet another issue was boundaries. Claire had already observed that Leila seemed calm and well behaved. And it was soon clear that Mohammed and Noor each had a good sense of self and were emotionally mature. They had their future ambitions securely in place and were prepared to work systematically towards them. And they'd already connected with a local mosque in Edmonton and become friendly with a couple of other displaced Syrian refugee families from Fort McMurray. All this boded well for keeping harmonious but professional relationships with Marisa and Alberto.

This was such a perfect idea in Claire's mind that she had trouble keeping it to herself and later that afternoon when she was alone with Roscoe, she told him what she was thinking. Roscoe was delighted. "I so sorry for them and I wowry about Mawisa. This is pewfec!" As Claire listened to his butchered words, she wondered how on earth he'd ever been able to communicate with Mohammed for whom English was a learned language. It had to be because of Roscoe's engaging personality and his endearing smile. That seemed able to make up for so much. She wondered what he could have done in life if not held down by his disabilities. Perhaps he could have been a very effective diplomat, somebody of the ilk of Jimmy Carter, another kind man.

Chapter 20: Now For That Other Problem!

The dinner went well that evening and the next day Tia, Jimmy and Alberto met with Mohammed and Noor Alfagadi and made their offer. It was accepted at once and the family agreed to move in and begin their new duties as soon as the renovations were completed. Tia immediately phoned Claire with the good news. After Claire hung up the phone, she indulged herself in a minute of silent gloating. But then it was time to move on with getting the next piece of the puzzle in place.

Marisa would still need more help because there were also the weekend shifts to think about although Hilda had agreed to work for a few hours on Saturdays. Claire had already placed ads in the community newspaper and hung up ads in the local drug store and convenience store and the Laundromat. She reasoned that a part-time position would be more appealing to someone who lived in the neighborhood. Within a few days, she'd received three replies and today was the day she'd arranged for interviews.

The first candidate arrived and even as Claire opened the door to her, she'd already dismissed her from consideration. The girl was young, skimpily dressed and chewing gum. Her air was both jaunty and faintly condescending as if she were doing Claire a favor to even consider such menial work. Claire was acutely sensitized to this attitude because of her various experiences in finding home supports for Jessie, but even if that hadn't been the case, the fact that this girl reminded her so strongly of Amy, an earlier 'helper' who'd proven to be thoroughly immature, unreliable and self-centered, would have put her off. On the other hand, if it hadn't been for Amy, Tia and Jimmy might never have gotten together—but that was another story.

The second candidate didn't appear to have any of these faults but she had others. And Claire had good reason to be wary of them, again because of her own past hiring experiences for Jessie. This was a sad, faded-looking woman of about 35 with premature lines around her down-turned mouth. She explained to Claire that her husband was out of work and that's why she needed the job. Then she confided to this new acquaintance of less than ten minutes that it wasn't as if he was looking very hard for a job anyway. Then she went on to tell Claire that her mother was ill and she might have to take time off on short notice to care for her but she was sure Claire would understand. Claire did *not* understand and the interview was a short one with Claire asking only a few perfunctory questions and stating that she'd get in touch in a day or two after she'd finished interviewing the other applicants and reached her decision.

By this time, Claire was feeling more than a little discouraged and she opened the door to the third candidate with a sour and suspicious look on her face, causing the person to take an involuntary step backwards and almost trip on the top step. Claire was quick to make amends and welcome this new person in graciously for two reasons. First and most importantly, she needed to make amends for her antisocial presentation.

Secondly, she could see at a glance that this person was a much more promising prospect than the other two individuals. Claire didn't know how she knew that but she just knew. It had something to do with her experience gleaned from interviewing the many young women through the years she'd met in search of the right person for Jessie at any given point in time and also, in the past two years, the dozens and dozens of individuals she'd interviewed in order to staff the Co-op.

The new person was named Amelia Costanza and she explained to Claire that she was hoping to find a part-time position where she could work from nine to three, four or five days a week. She had two children, nine and eleven, and couldn't come in earlier because she needed to get them off to school in the morning. Her husband was gone by seven each morning for his work so she could not turn to him for help.

Claire didn't respond to this directly but in her typical way went along a parallel path. "Are you of Italian background?" she asked.

Amelia looked mildly surprised by this rather inappropriate interview question but then answered readily enough. "Both my sets of grandparents emigrated from Italy and both my parents speak Italian fluently. I understand it but only speak it at a basic level."

"I asked because of your Italian name," Claire explained. "But perhaps it's your husband's name?"

"Yes, it is. My husband emigrated with his parents from Italy when he was a teenager. He's anxious for the children to speak Italian and has always talked to them in Italian. They also attend Saturday School in Italian."

"I also asked because Marisa, the lady you would be caring for, is Italian. She has had a stroke and is only now regaining some speech. She may end up speaking to you in Italian because she's forgotten the English words." Claire felt much better after she said this, feeling it went some way towards justifying her former intrusive remarks.

"I would like that," Amelia replied. "It has always bothered me that I can almost speak Italian but not quite. I could get out my old, Italian books and bone up."

Claire then explained the job to Amelia and how it might be of a temporary nature, adding that she could likely always accommodate her for employment at the Co-op since that situation, staffed largely by students, was very fluid. Soon it was settled, with the girl agreeing to come in for training the day after Marisa arrived home from the hospital, and contact information was exchanged.

Amelia had given her the names of two references but Claire didn't contact them immediately after the woman left. Instead she sat down in her living room with a glass of New Zealand Sauvignon Blanc wine and congratulated herself on a job well done. She now had sufficient supports in place to bring Marisa home.

Chapter 21: Further Adventures at the Hospital

That afternoon, shortly after four, Hazel phoned Claire and asked if she could meet with her and Tia to update them on something that had happened at the hospital and get their advice. Claire agreed, made arrangements to pick Hazel up at a coffee shop near the hospital and then phoned Tia.

"Hazel said nothing in the car on the way back to Tia's house except that she preferred to update them both at the same time. Tia was ready for them and they sat down in her small sewing room where they could talk privately, as Alberto and Mario were both at home.

Hazel turned to Tia. "You remember you told me that we must not trust anyone at the hospital?"

"Yes?" Tia said curtly, worried about what was coming next.

"But we aren't getting anywhere, are we? I haven't been able to find out one useful thing."

"Nor me," Tia conceded.

"Oh, I guess that's not true," Hazel hastily added. "We *do* know that the murderer is a woman, a red-haired woman—who's either a nurse or impersonating a nurse."

"Well, we know that's what Mrs. Barton saw—or what she thinks she saw," Tia corrected.

"I've cleaned her room quite a few times now," Hazel stated, "and she has always struck me as quite with it. And I often find her reading the Bible, the King James Version. I don't see her making up a story like that."

"Maybe," Claire acknowledged. "But our original point still stands. It's best not to trust anybody or rule anybody out. We've both learned that lesson the hard way." Claire looked at Tia who nodded her head slightly, silently acknowledging the hard and sometimes dangerous road they'd travelled together in pursuit of answers to various crimes.

Hazel debated with herself what to say next, but finally she decided to come clean—or almost clean. "I've met this nurse there, a *male* nurse with short brown hair so he can't be the murderer, and yesterday he asked me out!" Hazel said this last with a note of pride in her voice and then continued, "I've seen him talking to the patients a number of different times when I've been cleaning their rooms. He's always so gentle and respectful to them and seems to go that extra mile. It's pretty clear that he really cares about them."

"That's nice," Tia said perfunctorily but with a note of anxiety in her voice. "But you haven't told him anything about us or what we're trying to do, have you?"

Hazel looked slightly furtive and paused before answering. "Well, I did raise the subject of the murders with him thinking he might be able to give me some information. But then he asked me what my interest in it was and I *had* to say something."

"What exactly did you tell him?" Claire asked evenly.

"Oh, I just said I was trying to find out what people here knew about them to help some friends who were working on finding the killer."

"And did he ask you anything more about these friends?" Tia inquired.

"Well, he didn't ask me your names or anything. I think he knew I wouldn't tell him. He just wanted to know if either of you worked in the hospital. I said one of you did––but I didn't say where or give him any other information."

"Did he ask you out before or after you told him this?" Claire probed.

Hazel looked crestfallen. "You think he only wants to go out with me to pump me for more information?"

Tia jumped in quickly before Claire could respond. Claire could be rather insensitive to people's feelings at times and Tia thought she'd better take over. "You're a very attractive girl, Hazel. I'm sure he asked you out because he honestly wants to get to know you better. We're just trying to tell you that it's best not to trust anybody in situations like this. We've discovered at considerable cost to ourselves that people are not always who they appear to be."

"Well," Hazel said grudgingly, "I'll try really hard not to share any information with him. But I personally think he could be a very useful ally."

"Be that as it may, please just don't talk about the case when you're out with him," Claire requested. The meeting broke up then and Claire drove Hazel home. But all three of them were feeling slightly unsettled for different reasons.

Hazel's date with Mark Barrow the next night was all she'd dreamed it would be. He was sweet, sensitive, considerate and charming. Mark took her out to dinner at a small, cozy French restaurant where she enjoyed a seafood ragout with saffron sauce—but no shrimp. Then they went to a play he wanted to see at an experimental theatre, or so he called it. Hazel couldn't remember its name later when she tried to describe it to Tia and Claire.

The subject of the murders came up several times and Hazel found this only natural. After all, it was a really frightening thing that had been happening in the very place where they both worked. He did ask her the names of her friends, but she refused to give them to him. Then he asked if they were some of the other cleaners and she reflexively replied in the negative. She wanted this man to know that she had friends outside the world of cleaners.

When Mark drove her home that evening, he kissed her goodnight but it wasn't quite the kiss she'd been dreaming of. It seemed more clinical somehow. He didn't ask if he could see her again.

The date was on a Friday night and Hazel knew that Monday was Mark's day off so she wasn't expecting to see him at work until the following Tuesday. But all weekend and all day Monday, Hazel checked her cell frequently to see if he'd called. He didn't call.

On Monday, Tia called a meeting of the cleaners for 11 a.m. Hazel maintained the charade of having only a distant work-based acquaintance with her and she listened with less than her usual enthusiasm to Tia's latest ideas for managing the equipment effectively and improving cleaning techniques.

After the meeting, though, Tia asked Hazel to join her in her office for a few minutes, saying for the benefit of the rest of the staff, "I'd like to discuss something with you about the state of your vacuum cleaner." Hazel didn't appreciate this because it made it sound to the others like she'd been careless, but she understood why Tia had to ask her in that way.

"How did your date go?" Tia asked abruptly once the door was closed. "Did he ask you anything more?"

"He asked again about who I was working with on the murders and when I wouldn't tell him, he said he supposed it was a couple of my fellow cleaners."

"What did you say?"

"His remark kind of grated on me and before I could think I blurted out a negative," Hazel said ruefully. "I should've been more coy and just said something like, "Maybe, maybe not."

"Has he called you since?"

"No-o," Hazel replied. "I guess we didn't hit it off."

"Oh, well," Tia replied noncommittally. And the interview ended.

Chapter 22: Marisa Comes Home

Claire and Tia quickly forgot about Hazel's romantic problems. For the next two days, they were totally focused on getting everything in place so Marisa could move into the house next door to Tia and not have to return to the hospital. As seems always to be the case, this involved more complications and organizational hassles and compromises than they'd first anticipated.

Claire and Dan brought up to Marisa's hospital room the original wheelchair made for Jessie with a built-in lift and built-in commode unit. With the assistance of the hospital floor lift, they managed to transfer Marisa into it. Then they tried lifting her up and down in the chair sling and Marisa didn't seem to mind. They made some measurements so the chair and cushions could be adjusted to fit Marisa's body shape better and, after transferring Marisa back into her bed, explained that they needed to leave.

"We'll be coming back to take you home in a couple of days, Marisa, and the chair will be all fixed up for you by then so you'll be comfortable," Claire told her, and kissed her gently on the cheek. Dan slowly removed the various pieces of the lifting apparatus and Claire struggled to fit them all back in their special bag so she could hang it on the back of the chair and then they left.

"I'd forgotten how complicated this process was," Dan commented, as he guided the chair down the hall towards the front door. "The new combination chair the engineer made for Jessie is so much better and easier with its built-in lift and sling system."

"Yes, but in the house we won't need to take the lift apparatus off and we can probably leave it on even to go across the street," Claire replied.

"That's not the only problem, though," Dan muttered. "Do you remember how difficult it was to get Jessie's clothes up and down for toileting purposes in this chair using the net sling?"

"Yes, I know," Claire sighed. "But even if Jessie didn't need the other chair, we couldn't use it for Marisa. It has only one position—upright—and Marisa needs a reclining chair now that she's so stiff. Ideally, she needs a tilt-in-space chair that would support her legs in a reclined position. But to buy a chair like that and get the engineer to install a lift and commode and the built-in hard sling that makes undressing and dressing easy would cost well over $100,000 dollars. And now that Alberto has bought the house, he doesn't have the money for that."

"You know, Claire, I don't think it would work anyway. Having seen Marisa now, I'd say she's too fragile to be lifted like we lift Jessie."

"I was wondering about that," Claire sighed. "What I really wanted to do today was to bring Jessie's new lift chair up to the hospital to try it out so we could make plans for the future, but I knew what you would say—that there's no time to fool around right now."

"Which is true," Dan told her firmly. This chair will work as a wheelchair for her for the time being once we make the necessary adjustments, but I don't think it's really going to work as a commode chair."

"I'm afraid you're right," Claire sighed. She thought of all the planning and work that had gone into producing the two prototypes, how she'd imagined it changing the life of so many people with severe disabilities—allowing them to remain at home or at least to have their needs properly met in a hospital without wearing out their assistants in the process or ending up neglected and ignored. But there was still so far to go—*probably beyond my lifetime,* she thought.

Claire shook herself out of her reverie and tried to figure out how to solve the commode problem for Marisa. *That* was what she needed to focus on now. Then an idea came to her. "Wait! Do you remember that new commode chair we got from Alberta Aids to Daily Living for Jessie a couple of years ago? It never worked for her because it was too big and had too much padding in the wrong places. Do you suppose we could make it work for Marisa? Jessie's still okay using her old commode chair."

"It's possible," Dan agreed. "I noticed that Marisa is wider in the hips despite how thin she is."

"Do we have all the materials we need to make the necessary adjustments to the wheelchair ourselves?"

Dan snorted. He didn't know why Claire kept talking about "we" when *he* was the one who was going to have to do all the work on the chair. "I can do the mechanical part but if we have to reshape and re-sew cushions, we'd need an industrial machine."

"If we're just using the wheelchair as a wheelchair right now, that's not so urgent. If we have to, we can buy high-density foam from Foam King and get them to cut it to the right shape. We can worry about covering it later. I think we need to take this chair home, pick up the commode chair and go back to the hospital and see how well Marisa can sit in it."

Dan sighed but finally agreed that Claire was right. Fortunately, Marisa was still awake when they returned with the commode chair and seemed happy to see them. They went through the same measuring process all over again and then said their good-byes a second time and trundled the commode chair down the hall.

They headed directly for Camper's Village where they'd had considerable help in the past with adjusting Jessie's equipment from the very nice and accomplished seamstress who worked there. They showed her the pen marks they'd made on the vinyl-covered foam padding to indicate where it needed to be reduced or expanded, purchased the extra belts they'd need to be attached to the chair to keep Marisa safe, and left it with her with the promise that it would be ready by 4 p.m. the next day.

"Okay!" Claire said briskly, when they left. "Now we need to figure out a change table. I know there's some extra wood at home and we can drive to Foam King and pick up the foam for the surface and then we can go to Fabricland to get the vinyl to cover it and maybe I can get Fuji to put it together."

Dan groaned. "How do you propose for him to get that done in the next two days when he's already using every spare minute to do the renovations at Alberto's new house?"

Claire sat back and realized that Dan was right. *But how can we manage otherwise?* Then Claire remembered an email she'd received recently and pulled out her trusty iPad that she always carried with her. It didn't take long to find what she was looking for and she informed Dan. "Alberta Health Services is having a sale of old equipment at their main office and that's not far from here. They're selling off old wheelchairs and stretchers, the kind you have to step pump to lift up. We could get one of those. They already have safety belts and once we raise it to the right height, we can just leave it there, depending on how tall Marisa's assistant is. Anyway, raising or lowering it once a shift wouldn't be too bad. The sale's at their south side office on 99th Street, between 53rd and Argyll. Let's go!"

Dan didn't argue but headed the car in that direction. He immediately saw Claire's logic. "I can see how that would work and it would be easy to move around which is important. What about the side rail, though? That would make lifting awkward."

"Can't you just remove it? The stretcher is never going to be used for her to sleep in."

"I suppose so," said Dan, slowing the car down and turning around.

"What are you *doing*?" Claire practically screamed.

"You forget that we have the commode in the back of the van. We wouldn't have room to carry the stretcher as well. We have to take it back to the house first."

"No! There's no time. Just go to the store! It's closing soon! I'll figure something out." Claire pulled out her phone and started dialing frantically. In a few minutes, she turned to him and said, "Randy is going to meet us there with his truck so he can carry the stretcher. He'll come as soon as we make the deal and call him." Dan just grinned at her affectionately and kept driving. Somehow, Claire always found a way.

By 4 o'clock that afternoon, they were the proud owners of a second-hand stretcher. Later that evening, Tia meticulously scrubbed it with a bleach/soap solution and Claire mended the single tear in its padded vinyl surface with an almost matching color of grey plumber's tape. Prior to that, Dan had been able to remove the railing from one side without weakening the overall structure, but then he had needed to run to a local wheelchair supply store to purchase replacements for the tires, which were badly worn.

The next day, Fuji and Randy carried Tia's guest room double bed next door and set it up in the master bedroom. Tia had already purchased a new firm mattress and a memory foam mattress topper for it. She covered the top with a rubberized mattress protector and tucked in a fitted, queen-sized quilted cotton mattress cover over that. She had washed it in hot water and dried it on high in the dryer to shrink it to the right size, having learned of the shrinkability of mattress covers from previous sad experiences.

Now was the moment Tia had been waiting for. She lovingly made up the bed with freshly washed, very soft sheets and a duvet with a soft cover in lavender tones, her mother's favorite color. She imagined Alberto and Marisa back in the same bed tomorrow night after so many months apart, his arms protectively around her, and a couple of her tears fell on the clean duvet.

That evening, Claire was running through her list of final arrangements before Marisa's return. The commode, lift and bed were in place. And Marisa could use Mavis' bath, lifting system and easy chair when she was in the house across the street. A separate mesh and padded nylon sling had been purchased for her and she could share Mavis' bath sling for the time being. Claire checked her list again just to be sure, but everything looked to be in order and then she sat back with a sigh, feeling the tension lift from her for the first time in weeks. Marisa would be coming home tomorrow and it was all going to work out.

But, as seemed to be so often the case when those rare moments of peace and triumph come, they were not to last. The phone rang and even before she picked it up, she sensed it had an ominous sound. It was Tia.

She had arranged to take a few more days off from the hospital to get her mother settled at home, but that was not to be. Kay Shriver from the personnel department had phoned to tell Tia that she was expected at the hospital in the morning to deal with an urgent matter and it was not negotiable if she wanted to keep her job.

Chapter 23: Tia Gets Back to Work

When Tia arrived at the hospital, she went immediately to the Human Resources office to consult with Kay. "Your system has broken down completely in your absence," Kay informed her.

"What happened?"

"Anna left her locker unlocked one night and her vacuum cleaner was used by somebody else. It was left dirty, scratched, and with a full bag and a bent wheel."

"Okay. Is that all?"

"No."

"What else?"

"Anna was very angry and upset. Apparently, she took you literally that she was responsible for her vacuum cleaner. She came to see me in a rage and when she left she said to me, "I know what to do. I didn't grow up the way I did for nothing."

"I didn't know what she meant, but a few days later, I heard the security guards being called on the second floor and by the time I got down there I heard sirens. Anna had set a trap for the person who'd used her vacuum cleaner. She had deliberately left her locker unlocked and she went early each morning and waited to see what would happen. On the third day of waiting there, hidden in an empty locker, the vents of which she'd pried apart enough to allow her to see out, she saw Myrtle look furtively over her shoulder and then take Anna's vacuum out and remove the id tag from it. Anna told us later that she waited until Myrtle was loaded down with her pail in one hand and the vacuum in the other, and then she leaped out of the locker and attacked her. By the time the security guards arrived, she had the older woman flat on the ground and was choking her.

"What happened then?"

"Anna was distracted when the security guards arrived and before they could intervene, Myrtle reached up and clubbed her."

"With what?"

"The motorized brush attachment for the vacuum. Myrtle hit her hard and Anna is still in the hospital with a severe concussion. Myrtle was charged since the security guards were witnesses and she's been suspended from work pending the outcome. We don't employ cleaners with criminal records."

"Wow," Tia replied weakly.

"Wow, nothing. We're down two cleaners, the rest of them are all upset and disorganized and we need you. I'm sorry about your home situation, but if you want to keep this position you'll work here full time starting now and continue like that until this crisis is past."

Tia reeled back, her head swimming. *La mamma! How can I not be there when mamma comes home? ... Claire! Maybe Claire!* Tia sat back in her chair for a full minute before responding, her head spinning with conflicting thoughts and emotions. She realized suddenly that she really wanted this job. She *needed* this job. And when she thought of her mother coming back in that condition she suddenly understood something.

There's often a peculiar dance between mothers and daughters and she realized it was exactly so in her case. She wasn't ready for a role reversal. She was used to relating to her mother in all her dignity and competence. She couldn't now start treating her like a helpless child. And *besides,* she already had a helpless baby whom she was neglecting at this very minute. She continued to ruminate until Kay cleared her throat impatiently. She was expecting an answer and unwilling to wait any longer.

"Fine," Tia said weakly. "I'll do it. I'll get started now."

"Good," Kay replied curtly. She turned back to her own work, an obvious sign of dismissal.

Tia wandered off in a daze and found herself heading towards the cafeteria for an uncharacteristic second cup of coffee. Once seated, she called Claire and told her what had happened.

"Don't worry about anything," Claire said. "I actually think it's better this way."

"Why? She's my *mother."*

"I've spent more time with her than you have these past few months. I've seen the subtle signs of her personality re-emerging. I think—I *know*—that for her to come back to herself she must retain her sense of dignity. She doesn't want you to know her in this condition. It'll be better if you only see her for a couple of hours each evening and don't have to deal with any of her personal needs. You need to stay away and stay busy until we get all the delicate details sorted out and things fall into a routine. It's Alberto and me who need to bear the brunt of this. It'll be better for both you and Marisa this way."

"You really *think* that?" Tia asked, a sob in her voice clearly evident.

"I do ... and I *know* I'm right."

And suddenly Tia knew, too. She knew Claire would never lie to her or mislead her about something so important. A great weight lifted from her shoulders. "I've got to get to work now," Tia said briskly. "Please call me later and let me know how it goes. I'll keep my cell on whether administration likes it or not."

The next three days passed in a blur for Tia. There was much to be done at work, reassuring the other cleaners and regaining the cleaning standards she'd set for them. Tia worked at the necessary cleaning as hard or harder than any of them and she felt them respecting her for this and developing a new trust in her.

Hazel and Tia were very careful to minimize their communication, but managed to arrange a private meeting several blocks from the hospital one day after work. Hazel began by complimenting Tia on how quickly she'd managed to restore order in the cleaning division but Tia brushed this aside.

"What have you been able to pick up about the murders? Has anyone seen anything?"

"Not that I know of—and I don't dare raise the topic when Mark's around. I don't want him to start asking me questions again."

"We have to do something. We..."

"There *was* one thing, though," Hazel interrupted. "Janine, one of the practical nurses on the unit where your mom was, works a lot of night shifts. She said that before your mom left, she sensed somebody lurking around and a couple of times she saw odd shadows, but she hasn't noticed anything unusual at night lately."

"Claire asked me to watch out for the big complainers and to keep an eye on them," Tia replied. She specifically mentioned those with frequent requests to use the washroom. That appears to be the only common link between the murder victims and Marisa."

"It would be pretty drastic to kill someone because they annoyed you by asking to go to the bathroom too often. Especially when most of the care providers are very skilled at ignoring them."

"Well, we don't really have much else to go on. But one idea I was going to run by you is this. We do need to thoroughly clean the kitchen one night, wash the walls and so forth. We can only do that between eleven at night and five in the morning, so that would give us an excuse to spend the night here, which is when these murders are happening. You and I could do that together without raising any eyebrows. How about it?"

"Yeah, I guess," Hazel agreed nervously. "But how would we look if we were supposed to be in the kitchen?"

"That's just it. One of us could be snooping while the other was cleaning and if anybody should come in to see what we were doing, we could cover for the other by saying she was in the washroom or went to her locker for something. We can set our phones on 'vibrate,' enter our numbers on autodial and keep them in our pocket so we could quickly and quietly warn the other one to return. And we could also call the other for help that way if we were out snooping and saw the killer."

"Uh. Sounds scary. How about *you* snoop and *I'll* scrub," Hazel replied. "But however we do it," she went on, "I think we need a plan. We know all the people who were attacked or killed asked to use the washroom a lot and we know they were all on this floor, not in the closed unit for advanced Alzheimer patients upstairs and not in the units for ambulatory patients downstairs. That is all we have to work with and we don't have a clear motive."

"Oh!" Tia said excitedly. "I never thought about that, about them all being on this floor."

"Well, you haven't been around much lately," Hazel pointed out.

Tia ignored this remark which may or may not have been a jab, and instead offered a way to narrow the apparent target population further. "The people who've been attacked are not simply in wheelchairs, that is, they aren't just paraplegic. They're quadriplegic. They have limited or no functional use of their arms in terms of either strength or mobility."

"Hu-u-h?" Hazel asked.

"That means they'll never be able to function independently. Handicapped washrooms, for example, are designed for people in wheelchairs who can either do a standing transfer or a seat-to-seat transfer. They have some hope of being able to look after their bathroom needs independently but the clients who were attacked do not."

"Okay, but where does that get us?"

"We know two things now. The people being attacked are totally dependent and they haven't reconciled themselves to incontinency and keep demanding bathroom access. How many of the patients in the two units on this floor fall into that category?"

"I've heard a lot of them frequently asking to go to the bathroom, especially when they first come into hospital. Then after awhile, when nobody listens to them, they just give up asking."

"Then what we have to do is to identify the ones who don't give up asking, because from what little we know about the victims they would seem to be the most likely targets. How many of those would you say there are?"

"Well, I can tell you one who really comes to mind—Mrs. Kasper. She was the one from the waiting list who took your mom's place when she left and she hasn't stopped complaining since she got here."

Tia felt prickles up and down her arms. "Maybe we better see if we can come back and do the cleaning tonight so we can keep an eye on her."

"How are we going to do that? Admin staff has already gone home and we'd need permission. And how about your mother? Don't you want to spend *any* time with her today?"

"I'll spend some time with mamma this evening and she goes to bed early anyway. And as for kitchen access, I already discussed it with Kay and with the kitchen staff and they said we should just go in after eleven any night when we have time. We don't have to clear it with them and I was given a key when I was hired. So can you get back here before eleven tonight?"

"I don't want to go home. It's too far to just turn around and come back. And what about tomorrow?"

"I'll call in two of our substitute cleaners and security can open the locker for the spare vacuums for them. We can take the day off."

"Okay. I'm going to call a friend near-by and see if I can hang out with her until then."

"I'd invite you home but..." Tia said awkwardly.

"I know. That would be a *really* dumb idea."

Hazel was invited to her friend's place for supper and Tia agreed to pick her up there at twenty to eleven. Then she returned home to visit with her mother, nurse her daughter, bring back the breast milk she'd pumped and stored during the day, and to face the music with Jimmy. Mario and Alberto also figured in there somewhere and the whole confusing situation gave her a headache.

When Tia arrived home, her mother didn't seem to recognize her. Alberto was feeding her supper and Hilda was scheduled to take Marisa across the street for a bath later. When she told Jimmy and Mario about her plans to return to the hospital for a night shift, Jimmy scowled and Mario warned her over and over to be careful. All in all, it was a depressing and unsatisfying evening. The only good part was that she was able to nurse Marion before leaving and watch her fall asleep in her arms with a smile on her face.

Chapter 24: Two New Suspects

Once Hazel and Tia let themselves into the closed kitchen at the hospital, they both looked around with a practiced eye. A minute later, Hazel said, "I'd say walls, floor, grills and stove vent and the sinks could use a good polish."

"I basically agree," Tia said, peeking in the fridge and regarding it reluctantly. "I guess the fridge is not our business and we wouldn't have time for it anyway."

They got to work on the walls first, working together seamlessly. In an hour, they had them done and sat down for a quick break on the two stools set up at the sous chef counter. Tia and Hazel admired the walls. "They didn't look that dirty when we came in but they really were!" Hazel commented.

"That cream paint color can actually hide a lot," Tia explained. When they were ready to start working again, Tia suggested, "Why don't you get to work on those grills and I'll do a walk around to see what's happening in the two units, okay?"

Hazel nodded and Tia pulled out a small flashlight that wouldn't announce her presence readily. As she toured, she wondered if Jimmy was correct and she was being foolhardy. But then she reasoned that all of the victims to date had been helpless, easy prey. She was not. She felt the can of mace in her pocket and walked softly.

Hazel worked away on the grills using a power sander with a course plastic scrubber on it to wear away the worst of the burnt-on parts. She was almost finished and looking forward to washing them down and buffing them and then sitting back and admiring the finished look, when she felt a sudden tap on her shoulder. She jumped and turned around fearfully.

It was Mark and he grinned at her in what could be interpreted as a friendly manner. "Look at yo-ou, busy be-ee," he drawled. "Are you working here all alone tonight?"

"No, my boss is here as well."

"A-ah! That's your partner in crime detection, I'll bet."

Hazel just looked at him, flustered, and then she asked, "What are *you* doing here?"

"Night shift. Just on my break," he replied briefly. Then he added, "Hey, sorry about not calling you. My mom's been real sick."

"That's okay," she muttered. "I wasn't really expecting…" But just then, Tia came back in and asked in a peremptory tone, "What's going on here?"

"This is Mark Barrow. He's one of the nurses on the unit doing a night shift. He saw the light and just came in to check on what was going on."

Mark turned to her with his most charming smile and held out his hand. She shook it limply. "Hi, Tia. Hazel's told me all about you. You're her partner in crime detection, aren't you?" Mark asked, half humorously.

Tia just shook her head and said, "Pleased to meet you, Mark."

Then she turned to Hazel, but Hazel just shook her head ever so slightly.

Mark looked around the kitchen then said, "This isn't very dirty. What are you two *really* doing here?"

"You should have seen the walls when we came in," Tia replied curtly. All dirt does not show that much on casual inspection—and this *is* a hospital, after all. Sanitation is important."

Mark left then, stating that his break time was over. And the rest of the night, Tia and Hazel worked furiously. They had lost all taste for further snooping. When they left at

3:30, the kitchen was sparkling and smelled clean and fresh but with no residual chemical smell thanks to Tia's investment in some biodegradable cleaning products. But their investigation was no further ahead.

It was 4:15 when Tia finally crept into bed, trying very hard not to disturb Jimmy, but he reached out and put his arms around her.

"Why aren't you asleep?" she whispered. "You have to work tomorrow."

"I was worried about you, obviously. You, yourself, told me that there have been four murders at that hospital in the last couple of months and one attempted murder." Sergeant Crombie had phoned Tia a few days earlier to let her know that the second man who'd died had been smothered.

"That's why I was not there alone," Tia retorted. "And nothing happened anyway except Hazel's almost boyfriend turned up. Apparently he was working a night shift."

"Do you think he's a possible suspect?"

"I don't know. There's *something* about him I don't like but I just don't know what it is."

The next day Tia slept until nine, then wandered into the kitchen and greeted her mother with a kiss. Marisa was being fed her breakfast by Claire and didn't respond.

"Coffee's ready," Claire said cheerfully, attempting to cover up for Marisa's apparent lack of recognition, but Tia turned away and wandered disconsolately into the living room where Amanda had just finished changing Marion.

"I was just heading for the kitchen to warm her bottle. Do you want to hold her while I do that, Tia?"

"Don't bother, Amanda. I'll nurse her. I had to do a night shift at the hospital so I'm home for the day if you have things to do."

"As a matter of fact, I do," Amanda said gratefully. "Are you sure you can manage without me?"

"Yes, I had enough sleep," Tia replied, and then she added, "It's good to be home."

Marion nursed quietly but showed no special pleasure about being with her mother and Tia felt the curse of working mother's guilt.

By ten o'clock, both Marion and Marisa were down for a nap and Claire and Tia sat at the kitchen table discussing the home situation and the work situation.

Tia told Claire what had happened the night before. "Hazel really wants us to trust Mark and let him in on what we're doing but I didn't agree. He seems nice enough but..."

"Go with your instincts, Tia," Claire interjected. "It's all we have."

"But sometimes I think that I'm too suspicious."

"Better safe than sorry. There's too much at stake to have to worry about exposing our flank."

"But he could be a powerful ally as Hazel has pointed out and he's really nice to her, very gentle and protective. Apparently, the only reason he didn't call her back was because his mother was very ill."

"So he says," Claire muttered.

Tia just shook her head, worried and confused about the situation. "At least my mother is safe," she said, attempting to console herself.

"Yes, but there are all those others," Claire reminded her. "Do you think we have put the whole picture together well enough that it would be worth it to call McCoy?"

"Let's try," Tia said. "We have nothing to lose and we aren't getting anywhere."

They arranged to meet with Sergeant Crombie and Inspector McCoy at two that afternoon. Hilda and Amanda arrived at 1:30 to take over with Marisa and Marion respectively, and Alberto said he'd hang around or be just next door supervising the renovations if he was needed.

Inspector McCoy listened with an uncharacteristic level of patience and politeness as Tia and Claire outlined what they'd put together to date. But his response was not very hopeful.

"There are three problems, the way I see it," he said. First, we don't *know* that all four of the patients who died were actually murdered. The signs were pretty subtle and ambiguous in the two smothering cases. Second, it's very unusual to have three separate mo's. And third, we can't really be sure that the murderer is targeting quadriplegics only. The sample is still too small to know for certain. Finally, and most worrisome of all, there's no clear motive so there's no way to guess what direction he or she will go next.

"But we have to start somewhere," Claire pointed out reasonably. "If what we've put together is correct, then the obvious target is Mrs. Kasper as we mentioned. Is there any way to put a security guard on her?" But even as she said it, Claire knew the answer. There were just not enough police resources to spend them like this on a hunch—and not even a policeman's hunch at that.

Claire and Tia left discouraged and not at all sure what to do next. But at least they now had one possible suspect.

The next day, Tia was back at work. She was dressed more professionally than usual for the job considering that she still had some cleaning chores to get through that day, but a meeting with personnel had been scheduled for one. She was nervous and wanted to look her best. Tia stepped into the washroom shortly before the meeting to tidy her hair and freshen her light make-up. As she stood before the mirror, she noted one of the nursing assistants standing at the counter gently combing her beautiful long hair with a tortoise shell brush that looked familiar.

Tia quickly consulted her phone where Claire had sent her a picture of Marisa's brush and then spoke to the woman showing her the picture. The woman tried to leave but Tia took a quick picture of her with the brush and then grabbed her arm to get a clear view of her id card. "You'd better come with me to your nursing station to explain or I'm calling the police right now."

"I didn't do anything wrong," the woman, whose name was Iris, whined. "It was in the lost and found and nobody claimed it."

Tia knew this wasn't true unless the unit clerk Claire had talked to had lied. She took the woman firmly by the arm and headed back to the nursing station while calling Claire on speed dial. When she answered, Tia asked tersely, "What was the name of the unit clerk who told you Marisa's brush was not in the lost and found?"

"I'm pretty sure her name was Marcine. It struck me at the time as an odd name ...but what's this about?"

"Later," Tia said abruptly, and hung up the phone.

She hustled Iris over to the counter and was relieved to see that a Marcine was on duty. *There can't have been two of them,* she reasoned, and Tia spoke assertively to Marcine, explaining the situation. The woman blustered but Tia stood firm. Then she pulled out her phone and quickly dialed Inspector McCoy. Today must be her lucky day because McCoy was also available. She explained what she'd uncovered and advanced her theory that the murders might have been cover-ups for thefts and he needed to look into it.

McCoy asked to speak to the unit clerk and she paled as he spoke to her. Then she handed the phone back to Tia and McCoy said, "I've asked them both to remain there until I can get over. I'm in the middle of something right now and probably can't make it for an hour. Will you stay as well, please?"

"Yes, but right now I have to leave for a meeting with personnel on a separate issue but I'll be through by then."

"Okay, see you later."

Tia closed her phone and dashed off. As it was, she would probably be a minute or two late. But as she speed walked to the elevator, she couldn't help reveling in how far she and Claire had come in their relationship with Inspector McCoy. He appeared to have moved from automatically distrusting them whenever they offered a helpful suggestion to openly listening to them.

Tia hadn't been informed in advance as to what the meeting was about and she was surprised when she was introduced to the hospital lawyer in the room—Carl Lampon—as well as the former cleaning supervisor, Lena Dubrowsky. Kay picked up on the worried look on Tia's face and greeted her more warmly than she had in their last encounter.

"This meeting is about Myrtle Malloy: whether or not she should be allowed to return to work and—if not—what the legal repercussions might be," Kay explained, addressing the group.

The lawyer spoke then. "Ordinarily, if the reason for dismissal has to do with poor quality of work or unreliable or late attendance, there have to be at least two written notices on file and the worker needs to be aware of these notices and to have copies of them. However, in this case law officers witnessed her criminally assaulting the victim who is still in hospital with a concussion and a court date has been set for a hearing. Therefore, firing her should have no legal repercussions."

"But what about the fact that she was attacked first?" Kay asked.

"According to the report I received, there was provocation for that attack. The fellow combatant was protecting her assigned property and she did no actual physical damage to the assaulter."

"But I heard she was choking her," Tia interjected.

"Ms. Malloy was examined by medical staff immediately after the confrontation. The marks on her neck were very light, the skin was not broken, and Ms. Malloy was reportedly not more short of breath once released than would be expected from such an altercation in a heavy woman. Also, there was no apparent change to the quality of her voice according to witnesses familiar with her. It appeared that Anna Petrowski had been holding her neck to control her and not to hurt her. However, that is not to say that when the assault charge against Ms. Malloy is heard, this initial attack will not be raised again. But that will not be our problem here. The fact remains that when Ms. Malloy hit Ms. Petrowski, it could not be claimed as self-defense since she was in the presence of security guards and multiple witnesses and Ms. Petrowski was doing nothing more than restraining her."

"So the only question then becomes do we let her go or not?" Kay clarified. "Lena, what do you say?" Kay asked, addressing the former cleaning supervisor.

"I found her to be lazy, fractious and unwilling to follow directions. I would have loved a golden opportunity like this to get rid of her."

"Okay, what do you have to say, Tia?"

Tia spoke slowly and thoughtfully. She knew what it was like to be judged and found wanting. Her parents had experienced that as immigrants. "Myrtle *was* initially attacked by Anna and was undoubtedly in a frightened and agitated state. She may not have had as good judgment as she normally did. I agree with Lena's evaluation of her work performance, but if this proposed dismissal is based on her assault on Anna, despite the fact that it caused a grievous injury, I think we may need to take those factors into consideration. And at the very least, I think we ought to hear her side of the story before dismissing her."

Even as the words came out of her mouth, Tia couldn't believe she was saying them because she would have liked nothing more than to get Myrtle off her cleaning team. However, some stubborn sense of justice forced her to argue Myrtle's case. The room was silent after Tia spoke and finally Kay took over.

"Tia, I have reviewed Myrtle's file and I see you do have a note on there commenting negatively on Myrtle's attitude and performance and there's a similar note there from Lena when she was Myrtle's supervisor. This latest incident is Strike 3, so—one-way or another—I think any appeal lawyer would have to concede that the grounds for dismissal are reasonable and justified. What I propose is that we bring this to a vote. I, myself, will not vote to avoid a tie and also because I don't believe it's my place. Do you all want the vote to be open or would you prefer a secret ballot.

"Open is fine with me," Lena and Carl chimed together.

Tia just shrugged her shoulders and said, "You know where I stand."

The vote was then taken with the predictable results. Myrtle would no longer be the hospital's problem.

Chapter 25: Which Trail to Follow

When the meeting ended, Tia returned to the nursing unit to meet with Inspector McCoy. He introduced her to Sergeant Cordall from the Petty Crime division. "Why do you think this theft could be connected to the murders?" McCoy asked Tia. She explained her theory that the thief was afraid of being caught and resorted to murder as a cover up.

"Petty thieves are not usually murderers," Sergeant Cordall responded.

Tia turned to him. "I know that but something very bad is going on around here and there's no obvious motive for the murders so it seems to me we need to consider all possibilities."

"We don't need to do anything. *I* am turning the theft issue over to Sergeant Cordall. He will be in touch with you and Claire to give him statements about your mother's missing possessions and will follow up with interviews with the family members of others here who have claimed to have lost something. Meanwhile, Sergeant Crombie and *I* will continue with the murder investigation. I suggest you stick to cleaning and leave the investigative work to us from now on."

Sergeant Cordall couldn't hide his smirk and Tia left the interview fuming. Throughout the remainder of the day, she managed to ask several family members if they'd noted any items of their loved ones to be missing, explaining what her mother had lost. Several of them reported some missing items but they were quite ordinary: new socks or underwear, sweaters that were in good condition but not otherwise special in any way and one fairly inexpensive watch. In each case, the unit clerk had told them that the items hadn't turned up in the lost and found. Tia urged them to contact Sergeant Cordall who'd given her his contact information and they agreed. She could do nothing more than that except to phone Claire and vent.

"Why were more expensive items not taken as in your mother's case?" Claire mused. "At least it's being looked into—but I think what we need to do is to ask this Sergeant Cordall if he can contact the families of the persons who were murdered to see what *they* might have lost."

"Why?" Tia asked.

"I don't know. I just have a hunch," Claire replied enigmatically.

But something happened that night that was to wipe the smug look off Inspector McCoy's face. At three in the morning, a night nurse named Lorna was on her way for a washroom break when she noticed a strange light in one of the rooms. She peeked in the door and saw someone with a flashlight standing over the bed of Mrs. Kasper. Lorna just had time to register something small in the person's hand when her presence was noticed and the intruder rushed at her and hit her hard with the flashlight before running away.

About 20 minutes after Lorna had left her post, the other nurse on duty had reportedly gone looking for her. She found Lorna just coming to, and she was still very groggy. The second nurse immediately called an ambulance and while they were waiting for it to arrive, Lorna told her what had happened and what she'd seen.

When Tia arrived at work the next morning, the unit was abuzz with the news. Fortunately, Mrs. Kasper was okay so apparently the intruder had been interrupted before carrying out whatever plans he or she had. The nurse had told her partner that there was something in the person's hand, either a needle or a cloth—she couldn't be sure. She could not provide any description because the person had immediately doused the flashlight.

Tia was gratified to see Inspector McCoy back and looking very grim. Maybe he'd realize that he needed her help after all. But what help could she give him? Up to this point, she and Hazel and Claire had not really done any better than him. But maybe there was one thing she could add.

Tia marched up to McCoy and touched his arm to get his attention. He turned to her impatiently and she pulled him away from listening ears. "Remember, I *did* tell you that the next victim was likely to be Mrs. Kasper. If you want any more help from me, you know where to find me." And with that Tia turned and left.

Twenty minutes later, both Sergeant Crombie and Inspector McCoy turned up at Tia's office. "What do you know today that you didn't know yesterday?" he asked in his old sarcastic tone. Sergeant Crombie winced and grinned at Tia apologetically.

"Yesterday, I talked to several family members and a number of them reported items missing but they were all quite ordinary items, nothing as special as my mother's tortoise shell brush or her mohair cardigan. I talked to Claire about it and she suggested that it might be worthwhile to talk to the next of kin of the four people who were murdered to see if they'd noted any missing items and, if so, what those items were."

"Why?" McCoy asked. "What's the point?"

"I don't know," Tia replied somewhat impatiently. "All I know is that Claire's hunches have often proved worth following up. Do what you like," she said dismissively.

McCoy looked at Crombie. "Okay, coordinate with Sergeant Cordall and follow up with those families," McCoy said tersely, and Crombie nodded.

They left and Tia returned to the work she'd been doing at her desk, scheduling, budgeting, and arranging interviews with prospective new cleaners. But she had a tough time keeping her mind on it and finally gave up. All she could think of was what little progress they'd made and when the killer was finally going to succeed in murdering Mrs. Kasper.

Finally, Tia called Claire. She wasn't that happy to be interrupted since she was fully engaged in facilitating a delicate play of inter-communication between Marisa, Mavis and Bill. "I can't talk now, Tia. Call you later."

"Is anything wrong?" Tia asked anxiously.

"No. I'll explain later," Claire said, and hung up the phone.

Marisa had been sitting close to Mavis, and Mavis had reached out and clasped her hand partly around Marisa's wrist. Bill, observing this, had become slightly agitated and had voiced his concern.

"Mae-Mae … *my* Mae-Mae," he said quite clearly. Then he reverted to his usual flat, singsong voice, so common in individuals with autistic tendencies. "*Mae*-Mae … *Mae*-Mae … *Mae*-Mae … *Mae*-Mae," he droned. And then there was silence. Claire saw Marisa opening her mouth and waited to see what would happen. The silence stretched and then she noted Bill getting ready to speak again. She clutched his shoulder firmly, a cue she had developed with him as a silent warning that he should not talk.

"Ma-a-y," Marisa said in a hoarse whisper.

Bill shook Claire's hand off and loudly stated, "*My* Mae-Mae. Not *your* Mae-Mae!"

Claire glared at Bill but quickly changed her expression when she saw the look on his face. "In a soothing, low voice she said to him, "Bill, we helped you when you needed our help, right?"

Bill understood her and nodded his head.

"Well, now we need to help Marisa. We need to help her to learn to talk again. *You* helped her just now and she learned to say *Mae*."

Bill thought about that for a minute and then grinned. "*I* help Risa?"

"Yes, you helped Marisa. *I* tried really hard to help Marisa say 'Mavis' but she can't. But *you* helped Marisa to say Mae. Maybe if you keep trying she can learn to say Mae-Mae."

Bill looked suspicious and then said, "*My* Mae-Mae!"

"Yes, she is *your* Mae-Mae and nobody is allowed to call her that but you. But maybe you could let Marisa say it because she just can't say 'Mavis'. Maybe you can teach her to say Mae-Mae. Would you like to help Marisa, Bill?"

Bill grinned. "*I* help Risa. *I* teach her." He stood up and put his arm around Mavis' shoulder, facing Marisa but with his eyes focused just over her left shoulder. "*Mae*-Mae, *Mae*-Mae, *Mae*-Mae," he droned on and on.

After half an hour of this, Claire couldn't stand it any longer and she was quite certain that Marisa had had enough, too. "Okay, Bill," she said gently. "That's enough. When you teach people you can only do it for a little while before they get tired. Marisa is tired now. You can try again later, okay?"

Bill looked deflated and Claire called out to Alberto who'd been sitting in the kitchen trying to read a paper while all this droning was going on. "Alberto, would you and Bill like to walk over and visit Satou Botan if he's home? I can give him a call."

Alberto nodded, a look of relief on his face, and Claire made the call. Botan was happy to receive the visitors and Claire suspected that he didn't have much of a life outside the restaurant. Bill and Alberto left shortly after and Alberto later reported that they'd had a very entertaining time. Away from Claire's watchful eye, Botan happily demonstrated his knife juggling skills at Bill's request and he and Alberto both enjoyed the show. Then they drank tea together and ate some light but doughy Japanese cakes while Botan entertained them with stories of his cooking experiences in Japan.

Meanwhile, Claire attended to the toileting needs of both Mavis and Marisa, something she could handle on her own because of the availability of a ceiling lift and a change table. Then she transferred Marisa to Mavis' bed for an opportunity to stretch out her legs, relieve the pressure of sitting and have a nap. One of the biggest dangers for people confined to a chair all day is that they can develop bedsores and these can actually be life threatening.

Alone with Mavis, Claire worked hand over hand on some simple fine motor activities, wondering all the time what would actually be most meaningful and enjoyable for her. Claire struggled in her mind how to juggle her twin mandate for Mavis's and Marisa's care—rehabilitation and quality of life. She was glad she'd made the choice to withdraw Mavis from her day program but was feeling a new appreciation for the activities the staff there had developed for their clients.

Pointless as it might seem to have a group of adults sitting in their wheelchairs in a circle singing, or rather pretending to sing, child-like songs, it did perhaps create a sense of community and connection. Now Mavis no longer had that community. But surely the Co-op community they had created was a better alternative overall? Claire mulled over this, wondering if she'd done the right thing for Mavis or was just twisting things around in her mind so she could accommodate Marisa. But then she turned her mind back to her immediate job challenge: how to create the best life possible for Mavis; how to find the optimal balance for her between stimulation and rest; how to separate what Claire or other staff members would most enjoy for recreation from what Mavis actually enjoyed.

The house was very quiet now since Bill and Roscoe were both out and Marisa was across the street with Alberto. Mavis began vocalizing, a rare occurrence for her.

Claire spent a few minutes repeating her sounds in the hope that Mavis would echo them back, a first step in developing meaningful oral communication. But this ploy didn't work and Mavis' sounds remained completely random.

Claire fell back on a tried and true way of entertaining Mavis while simultaneously performing a necessary personal grooming task. She trimmed and shaped Mavis' fingernails and toenails and then painted them a bright, cheerful red. Then she wheeled Mavis' chair in front of a floor length wall mirror so she could admire the result. Mavis gurgled in appreciation and Claire had to content herself once more with that basic level of interaction.

Chapter 25: Possibilities!

Two days later, on a Thursday, Sergeant Crombie phoned Claire in the morning. He had tried Tia first but she wasn't in her office. After the initial greetings—he was very fond of Claire and always happy to talk to her—he got down to business.

"You were right, Claire. Items *were* stolen from each of the deceased and in all three cases they were something of special importance to them."

"Tell me, please," Claire urged.

"Mrs. Kravitz was a Polish lady and a devout Catholic. She had her rosary with her at the hospital. She was very attached to it but when her relatives checked through her possessions after her death they couldn't find it."

"Was it very valuable?"

"No. That's the odd part."

"What about Ellen Burbidge?"

"She had inherited an opal ring from her grandmother since they shared the same birth month, October. She always wore it on her fourth finger, right hand, and when her daughter went to the morgue to identify the body, she saw that it was missing. The ambulance crew swore it had not been on her finger when they'd arrived and the hospital staff claimed to have no knowledge of it."

"How much was it worth?"

"Well, her daughter said it was 18-karat gold but the stones were quite small. Probably a couple of hundred at most."

"And Mr. Hall?" Claire asked. She'd actually never heard his first name mentioned.

"Aaron Hall had a special lucky baseball cap he always talked about. He told everyone he'd been wearing it when he won a '92 Corvette and he claimed it was his lucky hat. It was not found with the rest of his possessions although everything else was there according to his relatives except for a nice grey wool sweater that had disappeared shortly after he came into the hospital."

"So what does Inspector McCoy think of this? Does he think the thefts have any possible connection to the murders?"

"He thinks the items from the victims might have been collected by the killer as trophies although that doesn't explain the theft of the more ordinary items from others. He thinks maybe there's another thief at work, separate from the murderer."

"I see," Claire said thoughtfully. "Well, thanks very much for sharing the information, Michael. I'll call you if I learn anything more."

"Okay, but stay safe, Claire—and tell Tia to do the same."

After the phone call, Claire called Tia and reported and they agreed it was time to get together with Hazel, review what they knew and decide on a strategy. Fortunately, both Tia and Hazel finished at four that day and Claire met them shortly after at a Starbucks several blocks away from the hospital.

Hazel and Tia both looked at Claire expectantly and she summarized what they knew: "Four people have died, one almost died after an attack and another likely would have died had the killer not been interrupted. Items of personal value, possibly for trophy purposes, have been taken from four of the victims and more ordinary items have been stolen from a number of other patients as well."

Hazel held up her hand like a schoolgirl. "Oh, we need to get Inspector McCoy to check if anything has been taken from Mrs. Kasper. Remember, Tia, your mother lost her brush *before* she was attacked."

"Good idea," Tia agreed, and Claire nodded her head.

"Okay," Claire said, in a getting back to business tone of voice. "We also know that all four of the fatal attacks happened at night and that they were all directed against completely dependent people on the second floor who were still insisting on using the washroom. However, there are two units on the second floor and there are victims from both units. How can that fit in with the notion that the perpetrator may be a staff member? Presumably, people are hired to either one unit or the other."

"That's easy," Tia explained. "The units are interdependent. Staff can go back and forth as needed, particularly if one side is short-handed. And the better women's washroom is in the east wing. The west wing washroom has a problem with sewer gas and maintenance has been slow about fixing it. Therefore, many of the nurses use the east washroom, whichever side they're working on. The perpetrator could go back and forth between the units and nobody would think anything of it."

"Oh, I'm glad you explained that, Tia. It's been bothering me," Claire responded. "Okay," she went on. "We actually don't know much else except the killer's methods have varied from smothering to toxic injection to death by poisoned cocoa to anesthetizing by dint of trundling a heavy oxygen tank and a face-mask into the room. Does *that* tell us anything?"

"Probably the killer wants to show how clever he or she is," Tia commented sourly.

"But wouldn't that make him a narcissist?" Hazel asked tentatively, drawing on the slender knowledge of mental health issues she'd picked up from one of the old nursing books that introduced some of the more common psychological problems. "And, if so," she added a little more confidently, "wouldn't that be a useful clue?"

"You may be right, Hazel," Claire responded with some enthusiasm. "And, as you may know (Hazel did not know), most narcissists are men so that could narrow the field further."

Hazel looked deflated and a little worried after this revelation but said nothing more. Claire asked if anyone had anything more to share and both Tia and Hazel shook their heads.

"Well, I for one feel like sleeping under Mrs. Kasper's bed," Claire commented, "because I have a bad feeling that the killer's going to come back very soon to finish off what he or she started."

"We have an old sleeping bag stuffed away in one of the lockers," Hazel said jokingly. "Some of the cleaners have been known to take a catnap once in awhile if they have a light cleaning day."

Tia laughed but Claire didn't and Tia looked at her with concern. "Don't even think about it," she growled.

"We have enough help at home right now and I could say I was staying at the Co-op because we had no coverage for Marisa."

"No! Too dangerous!" Tia and Hazel said simultaneously. Then Hazel added, "If anybody's going to do it, it should be me. I'm smaller and will fit under the bed better, Claire. And I know my way around the hospital so I could get away more easily, whether from the killer or the regular staff."

"Absolutely not!" Tia and Claire said together. "You're only nineteen years old!"

"Well, then, what *are* we going to do?" Hazel asked pointedly. "Claire's idea may be crazy but it's not *that* crazy because we're certainly not getting anywhere right now—and neither are the police. That killer is free to just keep on killing, as far as *I* can see."

The three of them looked at each other and finally Claire said, "For security we'd probably need to work in pairs."

"Too bad we don't have a fourth partner then," Hazel said somewhat sarcastically. Clearly she was thinking of Mark Barrow and the unwillingness of Tia and Claire to trust him.

"Well, if Claire and I had more reasonable husbands, then *they* could help us but as it is we'll probably have to lie, as usual, if we're going to do anything to flush this monster out."

Claire snickered. "Fortunately, we've become quite good at that. But how are we going to avoid detection by the nursing staff?" She turned to Hazel and Tia then, "And you *do* realize that if you were caught here after hours your jobs would be on the line whereas *I* do not have that problem."

Hazel looked worried. Tia just said, "On the other hand, if we catch the killer maybe we'll both get a promotion."

The three of them then stared at each other in silence. Finally, Hazel offered, "We *could* ask the police to do it."

Tia and Claire both snorted. "They aren't known for taking our advice and if we even hint at it they'll think we're up to something and put a stop to it," Tia explained.

"But what would you tell your husbands?"

"What would you tell your mother?"

"You first."

Tia replied, "Fortunately for me, Jimmy's out of town and Alberto went with him for a break so tonight is actually ideal for me. I can call Amanda and get her to sleep over and care for Marion. Mario is with her now since he's expecting me home at any moment. Mario's old enough to get himself to school in the morning. I'll just tell him I have urgent work at the hospital that has to be done tonight. That's pretty close to the truth."

"But what will you tell Amanda?"

"Oh, Amanda is one of us. *She'll* understand."

"On the other hand, maybe we should get her to come over and bring her frying pan," Claire smirked. She was feeling the old energy, the adrenalin rush. Maybe it was true. She and Tia really *were* bad. She looked at Tia and sensed the same energy sparking in her. Hazel just looked from one to the other confused.

"Next time you see Amanda just ask her," Claire said.

"What about you, Claire?"

"Like I said, staffing shortage. I'm going to have to sleep over at the Co-op. It won't be the first time and fortunately I have a change of clothes there."

"But what if your husband phones over and finds out you're not there?"

"Good thinking. I'll phone now and tell the staff not to answer the house phone. That way he'll have to phone me directly."

"And how would that work when we're supposed to be sneaking around?"

"I'll put it on vibrate and text him back. I'll tell him I'm in the middle of changing Marisa and can't talk."

"How does that fit in with all your talk about preserving Marisa's dignity?" Hazel asked innocently and Tia snickered. She was used to Claire's convoluted rationalizations.

"Part of dignity is being useful. By making this small sacrifice, Marisa will be serving the greater good."

"How do *you* feel about that, Tia? It's *your* mother."

"When Claire gets going on one of her missions she uses all of us. Get *used* to it."

Claire turned to Hazel. "By the way, what are you going to tell *your* mother?"

"You mean you want me along?" she asked eagerly.

"Of course we do," Tia replied. "Just as long as we're there to protect you. Like you said, you know a lot about the hospital that we don't know. That will be very helpful."

Chapter 27: Showtime!

The three conspirators drove off to find a quiet café where they could sustain themselves with a light but nutritious supper. Fortunately, they had only one car to worry about. Claire had driven Tia into work that morning because Tia's car was in for a tune-up. *It was meant to be!* Claire thought to herself.

On the way, they passed a 7/11 convenience store and Claire pulled in quickly. She hopped out of the car and returned a few minutes later with three mini-flashlights and three bottles of water. "Don't drink too much," she warned Hazel. "Once you get under that bed, it's going to be tricky to get out without being noticed."

Hazel looked at her in surprise but also gratification. "I thought you said it was too dangerous for me."

"It *would* be if we weren't planning to be nearby. All you have to do is try to sleep and if somebody approaches her bed who doesn't belong there, I'll phone you—put your phone on vibrate and sleep with it where you can feel it. Then all *you* have to do is grab him or her by the ankles and pull hard. The murderer won't be in any position to attack you and meanwhile we'll grab him or her."

"But where will *you* be?"

"You tell *me*. You're the one who says you know the hospital."

"You could hide in the washroom."

"Yes, but a nurse might come in during the night and see me there. Tell me some place he or she is not likely to look."

"Uh, you could hide in one of the clothes lockers in Mrs. Kasper's room?"

"If I couldn't fit under the bed, I certainly could not fit in there. Maybe Tia could." Tia winced when she heard this and Claire went on. "Actually, it would be torture to stand in that closet without moving for hours. And if Tia were needed finally, she would probably be so stiff she wouldn't be able to move. You, on the other hand, will be lying under the bed and at least be able to shift around a bit. Any other ideas?"

"Okay. Mrs. Kasper's room is right at the end of the hall and there's a supply closet just around the corner from it. It's quite roomy if we can get out the mop and pail and some of the other stuff in it."

"Where would we put it and how could we move it without being discovered?" Claire asked in a mildly disgusted voice.

"Isn't the room right next to it empty, Hazel?" Tia asked.

"Yes!" Hazel said gleefully, finally catching some of their growing fever. "I know that for a fact because that room is on my cleaning list when it's occupied."

"The stars are aligned," Claire droned, moving her hands like a fortune-teller.

Tia laughed but she realized she too was feeling the old energy. "Who's the lightest on her feet and least likely to drop something?" Tia asked, and she and Claire both pointed their fingers at Hazel.

"Is there enough room for both of us in there?" Claire asked, "or can you think of another hiding place near-by? I would actually prefer to have visual contact if possible."

Hazel thought for several minutes in silence. "If I remember correctly, there's a small room with an electrical box almost directly across from Mrs. Kasper's room. Were you shown it, Tia?"

"Yes, I remember it now. Is that the one with the cord coming out?"

"Yes. There was no outlet along that entire wall on either side and the cleaning staff had no place to plug in our vacuums so the electrician ran a line out from the box and right through the side of the door in the middle and then down the wall under the hollowed out door frame so he could put in a box on the hall side. And through that hole, we should be able to see Mrs. Kasper's door across from it," Tia concluded gleefully.

"But not as long as the wire's in the hole. We'll have to cut it," Claire pointed out.

"And how are we going to do that without getting either electrocuted or caught?" Tia asked.

But Claire had just pulled into a parking spot at the restaurant. She grabbed the keys, jerked open her door and ran to her trunk. In a minute, she returned with a strong pair of pliers. "Ta-da!" she said.

"That's all fine, Claire, but it doesn't deal with the parts about getting electrocuted or caught," Tia pointed out.

"I'm surprised that Kay didn't mention it to you when you were hired," Hazel commented. Tia just raised her eyebrows. "There's a very clearly marked on/off switch on the board for that line. We just have to throw the circuit and we'll be completely safe."

"And you absolutely know which switch it is?" Tia asked doubtfully.

"For sure," Hazel said confidently.

"We're going to have to remove the part of the wire that is sticking out once we cut it. Otherwise somebody will notice for sure. That part could be risky in terms of getting caught," Claire pointed out.

"I'll do it," Hazel said. "You guys don't know me very well yet. You don't know how sneaky I can be."

They continued to plan while they ate their supper and at ten o'clock their car cruised gently into a vacant parking space on the street at the back of the hospital. Hazel produced her key to the back door, necessary for when she had to come in early and couldn't go traipsing through the whole ward and risk rousing the patients. They crept in and found the area inside to be gratifyingly deserted.

Hazel retrieved the sleeping bag and handed it to Claire. Then she grabbed the pliers and headed for the electricity room. Tia went with her; rehearsing in her head how quickly she could rescue Hazel if there was an electric shock. They had both retrieved thick rubber gloves from the closet and Tia was gratified to see that Hazel's shoes had rubber soles. However, she need not have worried. The hall was again deserted. Hazel did the deed quickly and cleared the wire on the other side. Then Claire joined her with the blanket. Hazel waited with her while Tia went off to her supply closet alone.

Hazel would wait until after the 11 o'clock check before creeping into Mrs. Kasper's room and wiggling under the bed.

At 11:10, Hazel crept from the electrical room, listened outside the door of Mrs. Kasper's room for a moment and then slipped inside. After tiptoeing softly across the floor, she slid her sleeping bag under the bed and crawled in after it, wrapping herself up well. In only a few minutes, she was sound asleep, the benefit of being nineteen, flexible and in a dark, cozy space.

Tia also managed to doze fitfully, huddled into a corner of the supply closet with a pillow and afghan that Hazel had purloined from the staff room. Only Claire remained awake, hunched uncomfortably on the floor of the electrical room. Fortunately, she had her Ipad with her and spent her time reading a story while ensuring that the light from the Ipad was well blocked by her knees. Every time she heard the slightest sound, Claire checked the little peephole but apart from a nurse and the security guard passing by at different times, she saw no one else.

Two hours later, Claire finished her book just as the warning notice came on indicating that she had five minutes of power left. Claire shut down her Ipad and wriggled uncomfortably in her tiny prison, wondering how long her bladder would hold out. But suddenly, she was alerted to a wavering light outside her door, something other than the dim, overhead hall light. She quickly glanced through the peephole and saw a dark shape blocking out the open doorway to Mrs. Kasper's room.

Claire fumbled for her phone and pushed the automatic call backs first to Hazel and then to Tia. The shadow receded inside Mrs. Kasper's room and Claire stumbled to her feet and opened the door of her tiny space. Her legs were quite numb at this point and she crossed the floor clumsily just in time to hear a crash. The intruder was on the floor but quickly jumped up, banging into Claire and knocking her down as he or she raced through the door. Claire quickly righted herself and ran out the door in pursuit. She was just a couple of steps behind, close enough to reach out and grab hold of the person's hair, when someone else came out of nowhere and jumped on her, bringing them both down to the floor with an ugly crash.

By this time, Hazel was at the room door. She took in the situation at a glance, side stepped the squirming bodies on the floor and raced after the intruder. But the elevator door closed just as she got there and Hazel ran down the stairs only to find the ground floor door locked. She trudged back up the stairs in disgust and peeked furtively around the corner only to see the security guard with his knee firmly in the middle of Claire's back and his ear to his cell phone. "I got er," he crowed into the phone. "I'm at the south end of the hall second floor, just outside Mrs. Kasper's room."

Claire looked up then and, seeing Hazel peeking around the door, waved her back frantically. A minute later, the elevator dinged and Inspector McCoy strode out, followed by Sergeant Crombie. He took in the scene with a look of disgust on his face. "I *got* her!" the security guard burbled triumphantly.

"No, you didn't," McCoy replied dismissively. This person is my special deputy." He turned to Claire and asked her what happened.

"I was watching from that electrical room right there," Claire said, pointing. "I saw someone enter Mrs. Kasper's room and I came over to check. He or she barreled past me and raced off down the hall. I raced after her and got close enough to grab her hair before this guy jumped me. The intruder got away through the elevator before I could get up." As she said this, Claire saw Tia peeping around the corner and rolled her eyes at her in an effort to communicate a 'stay hidden' message.

McCoy, who missed little, sent the security guard back to his post on the main floor, and communicated briefly with the two nurses who'd come running when they heard the commotion. He was informed that Mrs. Kasper was fine, but understandably frightened by all the uproar. He led Claire to the end of the hall out of earshot of the two very curious nurses and said to her rather curtly, "Our car is out back. Meet me there, asap—with your friends." Then he and the sergeant left.

Claire waited for the nurses to enter Mrs. Kasper's room with some warming blankets and hot cocoa for both her and her equally upset roommate. Then she rang for the elevator and hurried Tia and Hazel out of their respective hiding places. Only when they were all safely in the elevator did she realize that she was holding the intruder's red wig in her hands.

When the three of them arrived at the unmarked car in the alley, Inspector McCoy gave them one of his signature scowls but they saw a tiny smirk on Michael Crombie's face. "Follow us to the station," McCoy ordered, and motioned to his partner to take off.

Chapter 24: An Alliance of Sorts

Tia, Claire and Hazel sat side-by-side at a long table in the large interrogation room at the station and waited for the two policemen to enter.

Hazel was notably nervous but Claire and Tia not so much. At this point, they were well acquainted with McCoy's tactics. They knew, for example, that his bark was worse than his bite, and that there were ways to work around his ego and to penetrate his weak spots. What they had come to realize was that Inspector McCoy was not crooked, lazy or cowardly—just rigid, obnoxious and vain. But in the end, he wanted to get the job done just as badly as they did.

Five minutes later, McCoy entered the room carrying a fresh pot of coffee. Sergeant Crombie followed with a tray of cups, some napkins, and a plate of rather uninspiring looking cookies. The two policemen sat down and stared appraisingly at the women seated across from them. Finally, Claire blurted, "Aren't you going to turn on the recorder?"

"Not *this* time," McCoy replied, "because I know from past experience it's not going to do me any good and also because I don't want any remarks I might make to be on record. However, Sergeant Crombie will take notes."

"Oh," was all Claire could say. The others remained silent.

"So tell me what the three of you were doing there in the middle of the night and what you hoped to accomplish?" McCoy began.

Hazel and Tia turned to Claire and she described their plan and presented the wig to him. She was expecting to be interrupted at any minute, but McCoy waited patiently until she was through. And still he waited.

Timidly, she commented, "It's too bad no one was watching the doors to see who exited."

"Oh, but we did have personnel on all *three* doors, including the emergency exit. We were talking to them on the phone while you were waiting for us in here. Nobody came out of the hospital."

"Maybe the person knows and is waiting for the police to leave."

"They're on until shift change at seven and then there's no point in remaining because everyone on the night shift will be leaving at once," McCoy replied. "I'll tell you what's too bad, though. It's too bad that amateurs jumped in where they didn't belong and scared the person off, probably permanently."

Tia blushed and Hazel hung her head but Claire replied defiantly. "I would have had the person if that security guard hadn't interfered. Couldn't he see that I was chasing someone?"

"He thought the two of you were in it together," McCoy replied wearily. Crombie had stepped out to check on the reconnaissance team again but came back in shaking his head, and it was now 5:30 in the morning. Some of the early morning staff would be coming in soon and others would be leaving.

"It looks like it's a bust," Crombie said regretfully.

Maybe we did learn something," Claire said with a certain amount of hubris. "If the person didn't come out, doesn't that mean he or she must work there and probably just sneaked back to his or her post? Now, the question is who can leave their responsibilities for up to half an hour and not be noticed?"

But McCoy had had enough. "In the interests of full disclosure, I'll say that we've had little success in our investigation of this series of mysterious murders in that extended care center. I'll further concede that some of the things you've uncovered are of value to this investigation. However, what you did last night resulted in more harm than good."

"What about the wig?" Claire asked. "Doesn't that help? Can't you get a DNA analysis from hair cells inside it?"

"Maybe and maybe not—and who knows how long it will take."

"The lab is always backed up. And, even if we get the analysis done before this case goes to the dead files, whom would we match it to? But, okay, let's assume we did get a match. How would we use that evidence in court? How would we explain how we got it? The chain of evidence is contaminated."

Hazel and Tia looked properly abashed, but Claire was having none of it. "You could check up on that person, get a warrant to search her house, find out about her background. The reason this case is so hard is that we don't have a motive."

"I grant you that," McCoy replied. "Who kills people because they want to go the bathroom? And I concede that you've made a valuable connection there that *is* helpful to the investigation—or would be if it has not permanently scared away the perpetrator."

"She'll try again. I *know* it!" Claire retorted.

"Why do you now think it's a she?" Hazel asked. "A man is even more likely than a woman to don a fake wig for a disguise."

"I was just able to cup her shoulder for a second when I grabbed her wig. It felt like a woman's shoulder—softer."

"Well," McCoy said grudgingly, "it's not definitive but it *is* something. Witnesses have been able to provide some valuable information from the briefest of connections with suspects." Sergeant Crombie nodded his head.

"Where do we go from here?" Claire asked.

"*We* don't go anywhere. *You* are to stay away from that hospital. You have absolutely no reason to be there anymore—and if all three of you don't cooperate, I'll have no alternative but to out your friends here to the administration which will likely put their jobs on the line."

"Hey, this was a one-off for me," Tia blurted. "I have a three-month-old baby at home whom I'd like to get back to sometime soon. And Hazel has plenty on her plate without trying to do your job—although we probably saved that woman's life tonight in case you hadn't noticed."

"That you did!" Crombie interjected, speaking for the first time.

Sometimes, Claire thought, *it's like he just can't take any more of McCoy's mean spiritedness.*

"Humph," McCoy responded. "Maybe so, maybe not. The security guard *was* right there."

"Her door was pushed almost shut. He wouldn't have seen anything," Claire pointed out.

McCoy didn't respond, but simply said, "Well, that's all for now. You ladies are free to leave."

Hazel and Tia breathed a sigh of relief and filed out of the room. Claire followed but with a sour look on her face. Claire was driving and she dropped Tia off first and then Hazel. On the long way back from Hazel's house, she decided to drive by the hospital on a hunch. She circled the hospital and drove through the alley behind it, checking for lights on the main and lower floors. Satisfied, she finally returned home.

Meanwhile, in a small storage room on the main floor of the hospital, a woman tossed and turned in her sleeping bag waiting for seven a.m. so she could report for her day shift.

Chapter 25: Time to Act

She looked carefully from side to side and behind her, too. Nobody was there. Nobody was looking. Why would they? You could barely see this door from the road. And it was a nothing door anyway. She slipped through and quickly locked it behind her. This was the trickier part—to get to her secret place without being seen. And then wait. It had to be tonight, but later—much later.

Meanwhile, at Claire's house, a strenuous argument was underway.

"Why are you going out again, after what happened last night?" her husband demanded.

"I have to go. It has to be done. She'll die otherwise. Maybe tonight. Probably tonight."

"And the police? Don't they know that? Aren't they watching?"

"They think she's been scared off because of what happened last night. They think she won't even come back. Too risky."

"And you think otherwise? Why?"

"I just know. Sometimes I just *know*!"

"And Jessie?"

"She'll be asleep by the time I leave. You won't have to do anything."

"And if you never come back? What about us? She killed one of them with a needle. What if she turned it on you?"

"I felt her shoulder. She's not that strong. I could protect myself."

"I doubt that. And why you? Why are you going alone? What about the others?"

"Too risky. If they get caught, their jobs are on the line. And Tia can't come anyway. Think about the baby!"

"Yeah. Maybe left motherless—like Jessie might be!"

"It won't come to that."

Dan looked at her—love, fear, frustration and fury rolling across his face. "Fine. If you insist on going, I'm going, too. Call someone to come in and stay with Jessie."

"No, Dan. I know the place. There's only room for one where I'll be. Just let me go—please!"

Dan looked at her. He loved her. This was part of who she was. He had no choice but to let her go. "I want a text every hour and if I don't get one, I'm calling McCoy!" He hugged her and walked away. "Just remember we need you," was his parting shot.

Claire was trembling as she gathered the things she needed. She hated fighting with Dan. It always left her drained. *I better take two energy bars,* she thought.

At midnight, Claire slipped through the back door of the hospital using one of the two keys she'd copied from Tia's set. Slowly, she crept up the stairs in the dark and used the second key to enter the electrical room opposite Mrs. Kasper's room. She carefully noted the degree to which that room door was ajar. That way if she was reading her Ipad to pass the time and missed the exact moment of someone passing, she would know if the door was different. Patience was not one of Claire's strengths.

At 2:15, she stretched and tried to work the crick out of her neck. *How do detectives do this kind of surveillance?* she asked herself, longing for her nice soft bed. Her bladder was just beginning to give notice and she gauged how much longer it would hold out. *If nothing happens by four, I think I'll have to call it a night,* she thought.

At 3:05, Claire heard a faint creak on the stairs. She stood up and flexed her legs, wanting to be in better shape for action than she'd been the night before. She heard slow steps in the hall and saw a shadowy figure moving towards Mrs. Kasper's door. Heart pounding, she watched the person slowly push the door open and enter the room. Carefully, Claire turned the handle on her room door and crept out and across the hall. But when she was able to peek through the door, she saw the glint of a needle and knew there was no time to lose.

Claire stuck the whistle in her mouth she'd brought and rushed the woman, grabbing her by the shoulders and blowing the whistle as she grabbed. But the shoulders didn't feel soft and the person twisted around, drove Claire to the floor and kneeled on her, the needle perilously close to her neck. Claire used all her strength to keep that arm from coming closer but it wasn't enough. The needle touched and then entered her neck. Frantically, she clutched the woman's wrist with both hands to keep her from pushing the cylinder in but some of the fluid entered anyway. Claire felt herself losing consciousness and at the same time sensed noise and bright lights. She wondered if this was the gateway to heaven. Was it like a carnival then?

Minutes later, Claire awoke to someone slapping her face and shouting at her. Nearby, the burly security guard was sitting on the woman who'd attacked her and apparently trying to talk on his cell phone at the same time. A nurse was standing over Mrs. Kasper, reassuring her, and another nurse—Hazel's male friend Mark—was the one who was slapping her. Just then, Inspector McCoy arrived and stared down at her. It was all too much to process and Claire passed out again.

It was seven o'clock the next morning, when Claire awoke again to find herself in a hospital bed with a drip in her arm. She was foggy and disoriented and barely recognized the haggard, hastily dressed man standing over her.

"Dan? What are you doing? Is Jessie okay? You're not going out looking like *that*, are you?"

He stroked her face. "You're going to be the death of me, Claire."

Claire looked around with a start. "What happened? Where am I?"

"Don't you remember anything?"

"It was a dream, wasn't it? Mrs. Kasper and the hypodermic?"

"No, it was real. And you ended up with the hypodermic in your neck—a lethal dose of morphine!"

"Am I dead? Is this how it is?" The room was fading in and out for Claire and she really didn't know what was real and what was imaginary.

"You're alive! Thank God you blew that whistle and help came in time."

"Oh. I just brought it to please you—because you were so worried," Claire muttered. Then she turned over and went back to sleep. A nurse had been standing by and she came over and checked Claire's pulse and blood pressure.

"She's okay," the nurse assured Dan. "But she needs to sleep a lot. You better leave now so she can rest. We'll call you if we have any concerns."

It was two days later, and Claire and Dan were just arriving home from the hospital. She was still weak and woozy and not quite herself. Tia and Amanda and Aunt Gus and her husband, John, were there to meet her. Amanda was holding baby Marion, and Roscoe was also there.

"Oh no! Marisa!" Claire exclaimed when she saw Tia. "Who's looking after Marisa?"

"Don't worry, Claire. It's all taken care of," Tia responded. "Dad's future tenant just got pressed into service early. And Noor is a natural. Mom loves her."

"Oh! Thank goodness," Claire replied, slumping into an armchair." Aunt Gus came over and hugged her, shoved a footstool under her feet and placed an afghan over her knees. Roscoe hovered nearby, patting her on the shoulder. "I wooied about you, Claih! You *scah* me. Why you *do* daht?"

"That bad person was after another lady and I wanted to save her. And I *did* save her, Roscoe." Claire turned to Tia, "Mrs. Kasper is okay, isn't she?"

"Yes, she's fine, but the whole hospital is in an uproar. Administration wants to know how two people managed to sneak in without being noticed."

"You didn't tell them, did you?"

"No. I was hoping to keep my job. But when you're feeling better, somebody from there is sure going to be asking you. I hope you can figure out some sort of explanation that doesn't involve me and my keys."

"I'll think of something," Claire said, but it was evident to all the people in the room that she was already fading.

"I'm going to help Claire into bed now," Dan said. "I'm afraid any further visiting will have to wait until tomorrow."

"But Inspector McCoy phoned. He wants to come over and tell Claire and Tia what happened and who the perpetrator was and why."

"Tomorrow!" Dan said firmly. "Two o'clock tomorrow afternoon. He and Claire can tell their stories then."

A few minutes later, Claire crawled gratefully into bed, just happy to still be alive. Ordinarily, she would have found it almost impossible to wait until the next day to hear the story from Inspector McCoy, but this time, for some reason, she didn't mind waiting.

The next morning, Claire felt much stronger. After Jessie left for school, she and Dan moved all her therapy equipment out of the large family room and organized a ring of chairs to accommodate everyone they were expecting for the meeting with Inspector McCoy and Sergeant Crombie. And by 1:30, they'd started to arrive.

Gus and John came first, followed by Tia and baby Marion, and Alberto who brought Marisa and Hilda and Roscoe over from the Co-op. Amanda came over with Matthew who was skipping classes in order to be in on this. And Jimmy arrived with Mario who'd been allowed to leave school early in order to be there for the big reveal. Dan was by Claire's side and Tia and Amanda hastily laid out coffee and tea and cake, finishing just as the doorbell rang. The two policemen entered and Hazel scurried in after them, having asked to leave work early.

Inspector McCoy began by asking Claire to describe what had happened up to the time when she lost consciousness. Before that, however, he turned to Dan and said, "I specifically requested your wife to stay clear of the hospital and leave the investigation up to us so don't think I have any responsibility for what happened."

"She didn't share that information with me," Dan responded, "but in any case, you should know her by now." McCoy shook his head, appearing to scowl and grin at the same time. It was quite a confusing message.

Claire told her story, glossing over details around how she gained entry to the hospital and the electrical room, but Inspector McCoy demanded a clear answer on that issue.

"I nabbed Tia's keys from her coat pocket on the way home the night before because I knew she didn't have to go into work the next morning and probably wouldn't miss them. That day, I had copies made of the two keys I needed and then returned the set to her coat pocket in the evening when I dropped by for a chat and she went to the kitchen to fetch me a cup of coffee."

"Oh, my gosh. I didn't even realize they were *gone!*" Tia responded, attempting to insert the appropriate note of outraged surprise into her voice.

McCoy looked at Tia suspiciously but said nothing. Sergeant Crombie looked over McCoy's head at Tia and smirked. Hazel gulped loudly. Dan came to their collective rescue by asking Crombie and McCoy to please tell them who the perpetrator was and why she'd done what she did, and the tense looks were replaced by looks of avid anticipation.

McCoy, being the perverse person he was, said nothing at first and Sergeant Crombie didn't dare break the suspense prematurely. Finally, he turned to Claire. "Who do you think it was?"

"Either a nurse or an LPN—she appeared to be wearing some sort of nursing uniform."

"Could have been, but wasn't," said McCoy and nothing more. Thirteen pairs of eyes stared at him with only Sergeant Crombie and baby Marion looking in a different direction. He finally got the message and gave them what they were waiting for. "It was the receptionist."

"The receptionist? Alma? The nice lady at the desk inside the main door or the one who comes in on weekends?" Claire asked.

"Alma Corian. The main receptionist."

"*She* was the only one who always smiled at me, who was sympathetic to my rants. She even agreed with my concerns that the residents were not taken to the bathroom when they requested and that it was staff stealing the items, not patients."

"Of course. That's why she did what she did."

"Somebody has to go to the bathroom so you kill them to stop the urge?" Aunt Gus asked sarcastically.

"The back story, please," Tia requested. "*Why* did she do it?"

Sergeant Crombie finally took over to everyone's relief. "It started a long time ago. Alma never married and she was an only child. She was thirty and unmarried when her father died and her mother became ill soon after. Alma felt she had no choice but to move in with her and look after her. The years passed and by the time she was 45, Elsie—Alma's mother—had deteriorated to the point that Alma couldn't manage her at home anymore. Years before, she'd put her mother's name on the waiting list at St. Jerome's Extended Care hospital where she worked and Elsie's name came up just as the situation was getting critical. Shortly after that, Elsie was admitted."

"But that was a *good* thing, surely," Amanda interjected. "Alma would have been able to visit her mother at lunch and after work and even before work if she got there early. Sounds ideal to me."

"It was and it wasn't," Crombie responded. "During her frequent visits, Alma often heard her mother begging staff to take her to the bathroom. By this point, Elsie was so completely helpless that full lifting support was necessary any time she was moved. What Alma observed was that staff rarely took Elsie to the washroom, either ignoring her request outright or else making some excuse as to why they couldn't help her right then. And soon Elsie was just put in diapers and taken to her bedroom to be changed when necessary."

There was an awkward silence in the room when Sergeant Crombie said this. Nineteen-year old Hazel was embarrassed to hear such matters discussed so bluntly and she looked around at the others to see how they were responding. She noticed a particular effect on the older ladies in the room. Amanda winced visibly and Claire's Aunt Gus shuddered. Marisa, who still wasn't talking more than a few words, closed her eyes tightly and Hazel saw a tear slip out. Alberto looked particularly angry and upset, thinking about the suffering and embarrassment his wife must have endured during her stay in that hospital. Claire and Tia just looked grim and angry and young Mario was looking at his shoes. Hazel noticed that Jimmy, standing beside him, was squeezing his shoulder and she remembered being told how close Mario was to his grandmother. Only the men in the room, including teenaged Matthew, showed no reaction, having schooled themselves in inscrutability when delicate personal matters were discussed.

Gus was the first to break the silence. "How long did that horrible situation go on before Elsie passed away?" she asked, her voice strangely croaky.

"Elsie died less than two months after being admitted to the hospital," McCoy said, taking over the telling of the story. "Alma told us that she'd been on the verge of quitting her job and taking her mother home to try to look after her on her own when she got a phone call at six o'clock one morning, informing her that her mother had passed away during the night."

"*Why* did she die?" Hazel asked, immediately suspicious.

"Nobody knows and there was no autopsy. The attending doctor just put it down to heart failure."

"Was Alma satisfied with that diagnosis?" Dan asked.

"She didn't make it clear," McCoy responded. "It sounded like Alma had been so upset and disoriented by the loss of her mother that she didn't even think to question the diagnosis at the time. But later, when she was able to think more clearly, she decided that her mother had died of a broken heart because of being deprived of her dignity and self-control. And *that's...*"

"So *that's* why she did it, why she killed those other people!" Mario interjected excitedly. "She was *saving* them from that!"

McCoy turned towards Mario in surprise. "That's right," McCoy responded curtly, obviously miffed that his punch line had been stolen.

"But I *knew* her!" Claire blurted. "She was the only one in that hospital who was always nice to me—even after I virtually accused the staff of the theft of Marisa's tortoise shell hair brush."

"And when I went to the desk to tell her that my mother was not returning to that place and I was there to collect her possessions, she just smiled at me. She was really nice about it," Tia added.

"That makes sense in a certain way," Crombie mused. "She *said* that she didn't like killing people. It was only to protect their dignity that she did it. With your mother gone, that was one less person she'd have to worry about."

"But she was always smiling. Every time I went in there, she was smiling," Claire said. "But," she added, speaking slowly, "come to think about it, it never seemed like she was smiling with her eyes. They always looked kind of tight and blank."

"She's had a history of mental health problems—three hospital admissions in the last fifteen years," McCoy stated baldly, implying that that should be sufficient explanation.

Sergeant Crombie looked troubled and jumped in at that point, despite a warning glare from McCoy. "She hasn't had a good life. She told me about it: —all those years of looking after her sick mother, passing up her chance to marry and have children or even to have a decent career— and then only to be forced into placing her in that hospital and seeing all the work she'd devoted her life to being ignored and gradually destroyed though what looked to her like cold indifference. It's hard to blame her for deciding that death was better for people in that position instead of what she saw to be a living hell."

"Murder is murder," McCoy said coldly. "She'll have to pay."

"She'll end up in a mental hospital and maybe she'll find somebody there to look after so she can expiate her guilt. She must have felt terrific guilt, leaving her mother to that fate," Claire mused.

"Pardon me for not feeling so charitable since she almost *killed* my mother," Tia responded, rather hotly.

"Well, it's all over now and things can get back to normal," Jimmy said. "When are you going to resign from that job there, Tia?"

Tia just looked at him and said, "That's a discussion we'll have in private."

"What about you, Claire?" Dan asked. "Is your thirst for adventure quenched for awhile?"

Claire looked at him thoughtfully and considered her life. Dan was so patient with her. He put up with so much and he certainly deserved a break from dealing with the fallout from her wild adventures. But, more than that, Claire thought about the things she'd yet to do at the Co-op: work on expanding employment and community opportunities for both Bill and Roscoe, develop a proper, home-based day program for Mavis, make life rich and meaningful again for Marisa and Alberto—and that meant returning to the never-ending wheelchair project and finally perfecting it so when Marisa was a bit better they could travel a little, at least locally and with an assistant."

"Oh, I have plenty to do and I don't think I'm going to be bored any time soon."

Tia rolled her eyes at this and then said, "Of course, if another murder drops in our laps we'll just have to deal with it."

Jimmy shook his head in disgust, Dan looked stoical and McCoy responded with a snarl, "You will *never* have to deal with another murder. That is *not* your job." Then he looked at Crombie and rose to leave.

There were many knowing smiles in the room as the group of friends watched the policemen's departing backs.

THE END

ABOUT THE AUTHOR

In her private life, Emma and her husband, Joe Pivato, have raised three children—the youngest, Alexis, having multiple challenges. Their efforts to organize the best possible life for her have provided some of the background context for this book and others in the Claire Burke series. The society that the Pivatos have formed to support Alexis in her adult years is described at http://www.homewithinahome.com/Main.html.

Emma's other cozy mysteries in the Claire Burke series are entitled *Blind Sight Solution, The Crooked Knife, Roscoe's Revenge, Jessie Knows,* and *Murder on Highway 2.*

APPENDIX

The Dignity Chair
Patent Number: US 8,622,412 B2

Many years ago, I devised a way to have a commode unit built into our daughter's wheelchair and because of that, my husband and I have been able to travel with her extensively despite the fact that she has no functional use of any of her limbs and needs to be fully supported while in a seated position. But as she grew it became more difficult and finally impossible to do all the lifting and transferring necessary for the toileting process, so I worked with an engineer to see if a lift and sling could be built into her chair. The goal was to be able to do the necessary undressing, cleaning and redressing while in the lift position. Public washrooms do not provide adult-sized change tables, nor the privacy required to use them with dignity. Also, lifting her was no longer an option.

Initially, I assumed that a commercially available toileting sling would work with the lift but I was wrong. These soft slings, made of padded netting, keep the legs close together, preventing dressing and undressing in the lift position. To accommodate those needs, the sling would have to be hard, not soft, so the legs could be lifted separately and the support system, while lifting, would have to keep the middle section of the body free.

As I worked away on the project and talked to various people in the process, I became aware of physically dependent seniors who had to leave their homes and go into a care setting only because their toileting needs could not be managed in the home setting. But even when they went into extended care settings, all the lifting and transferring necessary often meant that staff could not accommodate their toileting needs in a timely manner and they were soon forced into incontinence. I wanted to help these people, too.

But developing an adapted wheelchair to meet the needs of seniors with this level of disability involved a new challenge—protecting the fragile bones that come with age. Thus the sling needed to provide adequate support for the user while at the same time widely distributing the pressure of the lift system so as not to put too much stress on the ribs. This is how it works. A 6-inch wide elastic belt holds the person snuggly against the back of the chair which then lifts up, supporting the upper body. To provide the lower body support, two comfortably-padded leg cuffs, normally retracted into the chest supports on each side of the chair, extend out when needed, supporting the legs right above the knee. Thus, the entire body is free from the base of the spine to the knees and clothing can readily be adjusted up and down. The diagrams below show the chair in both the raised and regular positions and when raised the seat cushion is removed to reveal the commode unit beneath.

Pivato 207

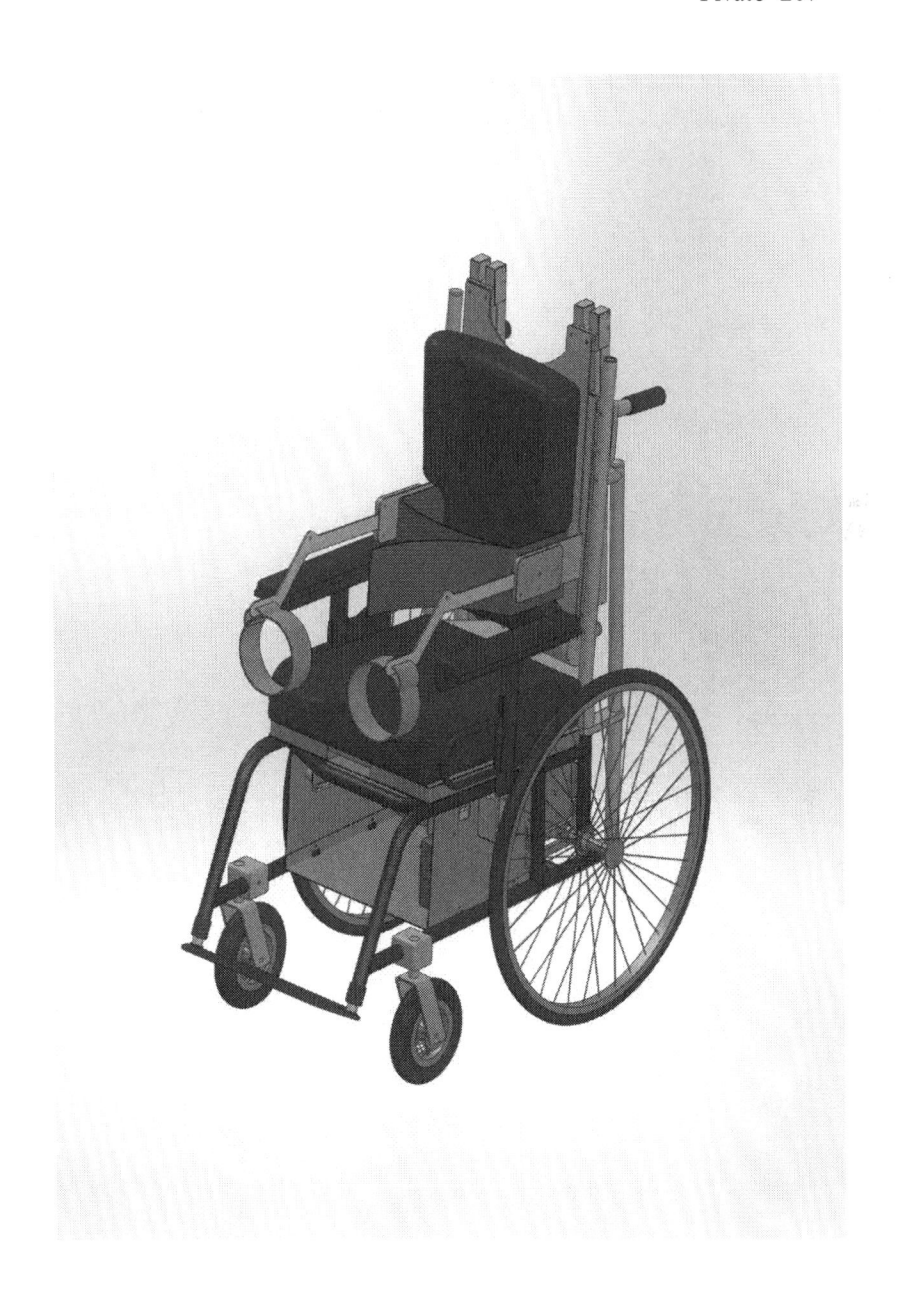

208 *Deadly Care*

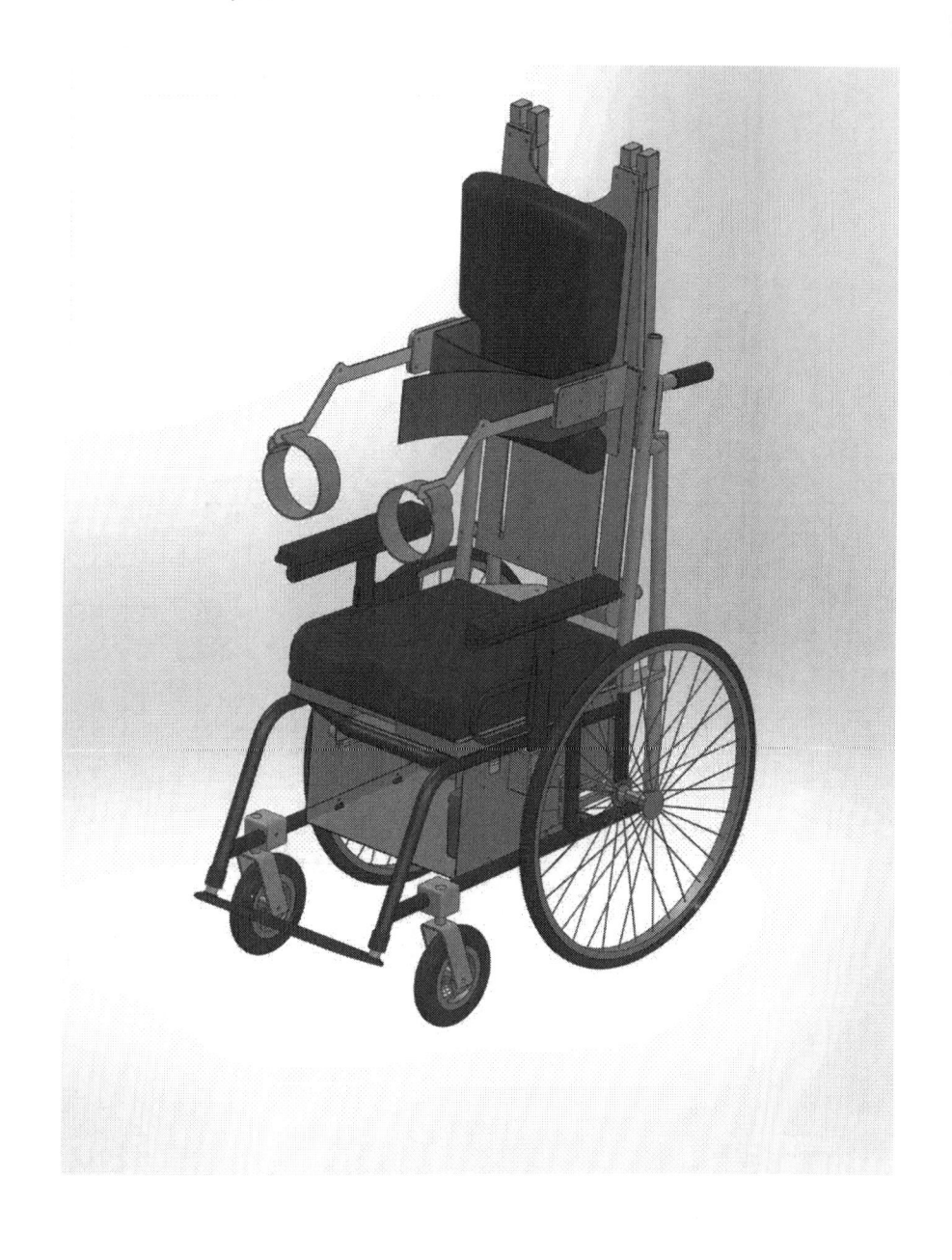

The model works well but the current prototype is built into an upright wheelchair, i.e. one that does not collapse and therefore has no crossbars underneath which would interfere with building in the commode unit. The seniors I am talking about would do best with a tilt-in-space wheelchair. That chair model functions like a small-scale movable recliner. The user can lean back with their feet up in a comfortable position in it. This is the chair our daughter now has because she has experienced further deterioration since her adapted upright chair was developed. The engineer I have been working with has examined Alexis's new chair carefully and is satisfied that he can build a lift and commode unit into it and also can further streamline and improve the lifting and sling devices.

Thus, as with all new inventions, there is much room for improvement. However, the adapted wheelchair described here or something equivalent to it is sorely needed. Seniors, who have lost their capacity to function independently and, because of existing logistics of care, who have also lost their dignity, could benefit greatly. So could people like my daughter whose severe disabilities mean that she can offer little back to society but her smile—and her capacity to use a toileting system with proper support. But inventing something new is an expensive process.

My wish is that others who have the power and the purse strings would pursue this idea. The humanitarian benefit would be great but there are also possible financial benefits such as reduced staffing. One person could safely, quickly and efficiently operate this device, whereas two staff are now required at all times to operate a floor lift. Reduction in diaper use and stress on the landfill would be both economic and ecological benefits. Making it possible for wheelchair-bound individuals to be raised up at times to talk to others at eye level would be psychologically beneficial to them. And alleviating sitting pressure through frequent lifts could prevent or minimize pressure sores—a major health concern for people confined to wheelchairs.

But most of all, such a chair would help immeasurably to preserve people's dignity. In this day of laudable efforts not to bully, offend or degrade others in any way, shape or form, surely this is a cause that needs to be considered.

Made in the USA
Columbia, SC
29 November 2020